AF261535

THE *UNCONVENTIONAL* CONVENTION

Story by
D.L. Roberts

Copyright 1995
by D. L. Roberts
All rights reserved

Dedication: To all of the people who have watched a political convention and who have laughed.

THE *UNCONVENTIONAL* CONVENTION

Story by D.L. Roberts

CHAPTER 1:
An Unconventional Convention

"This is a love story," said the doe-eyed, voluptuous blonde, clenching a microphone and addressing the TV camera as hundreds of people in the background converged slowly and steadily, like sheep grazing on a hillside, in one direction, toward the narrow entrance to the convention hall. Wearing the patriotic colors of red, white and blue and carrying signs with political slogans and candidate identifications, the people in the crowd proceeded along an aisle of camera equipment and television reporters.

Charla Willow, the attractive superstar of the national tabloid show called "Sensations," continued her report. She was an expert at furnishing a curiosity "hook" to draw viewers.

"This is a love story," she repeated, moving closer to the camera until only her gorgeous face was framed and she could see her reflection in the lens. Charla's broadcasting philosophy was to treat the camera as a lover. She moved closer, sensuously beckoning to the viewers to stay with her as she explained.

"This is a love story about a Democrat from Wyoming and Republican from New Jersey who fall in love in the midst of a great and glorious political drama. A love story that you have never heard before. A love story that will capture your heart and make you yearn for more." Charla paused, smiling, and then added, "And I will bring all of it to you during this exciting convention of the new third party, the political party called Ameriminds, as it chooses candidates for president and vice president in this great city of Normal, Kansas."

"Got it," Joey the strapping cameraman declared. Charla then relaxed as Joey approached her, saying, "Great hook, Charla. I don't know how you do it, but that's a great angle on this thing. How'd you find them?"

Charla winked and threw her arms up around Joey's muscular neck, whispering, "That's our next job. We've got to find them, bring them together, and give the public what it wants."

Surprised, Joey responded awkwardly. "You...We...have to find them?" The smiling Charla nodded. Joey continued, "Not again, Charla! We had a heck of time finding the radio talk show host who gave up his hateful comments for a life as a TV evangelist." Joey paused and scratched the top of his head. "Or was that a TV evangelist who gave up his hateful comments for a life as a radio talk show host?" Joey shrugged, continuing, "And remember the difficult time we had trying to locate a dysfunctional family of snowmobiling nudists?!"

"But we found them, and the ratings went through the mirror on the ceiling," Charla stated.

"A Republican from New Jersey, sure. But in love? I've known a lot of Republicans and one thing is for sure, love is way down on their list, below capital gains tax cuts and nasal decongestion. And why a Democrat from Wyoming of all places? That's about as rare as a music video with a plot."

"That's what makes it so intriguing," Charla replied. "And we need to find a cowboy, with boots, a tall-dark-silent type. Handsome would be a plus. Or folksy. You check out the New Jersey delegation for the woman. I'll get to the Wyoming delegation. Then I'll meet you back here in time for the taping of the next show."

Closer to the convention entrance, another reporter, Mike Troy of the TV news division of United General Homogenized, known mainly as "UGH News," began his report.

"A steady stream of people is coming together on this first historical day of this new party and new convention. Will it be the beginning of something big or something not so big? A tiger that roars or a bug in the car grill of life?"

Harry Hooper, one of the plain-clothes security police at the convention, equipped with a walkie-talkie, beeper, a hidden shoulder holster and revolver, and a clove of garlic, listened to the UGH News report near the door as he sternly studied the crowd. From crazy hat to crazy hat, the delegates seemed as normal as could be expected. Hooper took off his sunglasses and suspiciously eyed the delegates until his line of vision fell upon a hat-less, long-haired, young man in a crumpled, oversized, yellow raincoat. The ragged edges of the raincoat flapped above the tops of scuffed hiking shoes. The young man darted quickly through the crowd.

Hooper had reason to be suspicious about someone wearing a raincoat. It was June, and the weather was hot and dry.

Hooper moved slowly into the crowd, keeping his eyes fixed upon the young man, whose head was bowed and face was sober. In his head, Hooper heard music similar to the music in the movie "Jaws" to alert viewers to the presence of a shark. He crossed in front of an Alaska man carrying a sign for a realty company. He darted around a Michigan delegate wearing a wolverine costume. A California woman wearing a hat with a large, stuffed-toy banana temporarily blocked Hooper's passage. At that point, Hooper was distracted by the appearance of the bombshell TV personality Charla Willow and consequently he lost sight of the figure in the raincoat who disappeared quickly within the massive tide of people. Hooper lifted his head and began to jump in the air. His efforts to regain visual contact were fruitless, except for a brief sighting of the big banana.

UGH news reporter Mike Troy sent the broadcast up to Chester Mega, the gray-haired veteran anchorman, who was sitting behind a desk in a small TV cubicle that was perched high above the convention floor where delegates were milling. Over Chester's right shoulder, the distant speaker's podium and part of the giant TV screen could be seen by UGH viewers. The huge convention hall, decorated with patriotic ribbons and balloons, was expected to accommodate nearly 3,000 people--delegates and their families, visiting politicians, members of the news media, convention workers, assorted convention groupies and others--on the final evening of the four-day event.

"Good evening, ladies and gentlemen, and welcome to the UGH News convention coverage this third day of June. I'm Chester Mega, and from this balcony box, you and I will see the nomination of a new third party presidential candidate." The newscaster loosened his tie, continuing, "This is history in the making. And we will be witnesses." He chuckled, "Hopefully, we won't be called to testify." He turned in his chair and the camera followed his gaze down to the convention floor. "A little background about this event. Ameriminds is the name of the new third party--a name that stands for 'American minds' as some party leaders explain. It is a party of American minds coming together, a party constructed from a wide variety of ideas, both conservative and liberal, according to its party members. The leading party candidates are Ross Nebulan of Illinois, Andrew Chalk of Pennsylvania, Joyce Hyphen Martindale of Texas, and Josh Deaver of Missouri. Let's go now down to the platform as Sydney Paine, the party chairman, calls the convention to order."

Sydney Paine, a large man carrying a large gavel, waddled to the speaker's lectern. Puffing to catch his breath, Paine hammered the gavel several times, though most of the noisy delegates on the convention floor remained oblivious to his presence and continued to mill.

He paused, then shouted, "I call this convention to order." There was a sprinkling of applause and cheers. "I am happy to be here..."

Chester broke in, "Well, this is it, viewers. The first Ameriminds convention is under way. We will continue convention coverage after this commercial break." The TV monitor displayed a colorful graphic about UGH News election coverage, followed by several commercials.

COMMERCIAL: A car salesman slowly walked through his large lot. "We've got the car to meet your needs. We've got the car to fulfill your fantasy. Our cars are products of cutting edge global markets. The engines are built in Japan, the frames come from Mexico, the dashboards are designed in Indonesia, the tires are from Venezuela, and the windshield wipers are made in Sri Lanka. But most important of all, the air freshener that you see hanging from the inside mirror is a product from the good, old U.S. of A. Be sure and stop by Ted's Global Automotive City, a place where the world works together and for about $1.47 an hour, too." The salesman held up a small American flag. "And get this beautiful miniature American flag for your car antenna, absolutely free, just for visiting." The salesman opened the passenger door, and pulled a Bible out of the glove compartment. "And remember, there's a Bible in every glove compartment." He smiled, "Come in today. And ask about our 30-mile guarantee."

SECOND COMMERCIAL: A sweet, young woman was softly humming as she applied Make-Me-Happy Roll-on Deodorant to her underarms. Then she danced around the room, singing, "Make-Me-Happy sure makes me happy. And it makes Freddie happy, too. And Bob. And George, Arnold, Roger, Orville, and Clay." She blew a kiss, sensuously saying, "And how about you?"

THIRD COMMERCIAL: A talk show host provided a quick preview of an upcoming program. "Hedgehogs are being called the 'pets of the '90s. Why are Hollywood celebrities finding love in small, spiny packages? Is a hedgehog in your future? Join me, Calamity Jane McLaine, on 'Talk Until We Drop' this Monday on your local channel. Celebrities and their hedgehogs. Don't miss it."

The TV broadcast returned to Chester Mega at the UGH news desk. "Welcome back to the Ameriminds convention. Chester Mega here. And I will be joined through this event by a top-notch news team of Hank Midland, Saphira Pitchfork, Trixie Spaniel, Mike Troy, and Bella Wing. We will also gain some political insights from our election analysts Herman Merdell and Frank Fink. But right now, let's go down to the election floor, with the Pennsylvania delegation, as Hank Midland speaks with Cassie Chalk, the wife of major candidate Andrew Chalk. Hank, are you there?"

Responding promptly, Hank answered, "Yes, Chester, I have with me Cassie Chalk." The camera shows Hank, with a microphone and electronic head-gear, with Mrs. Chalk. "Hi, everyone," said the smiling Mrs. Chalk.

Hank continued, "Mrs. Chalk, are you excited about today?"

"Oh, I'm excited about anytime."

"Well, I was referring to the convention. Do you think your husband has enough votes to take the nomination?"

Chuckling as the Pennsylvania crowd cheered, she replied confidently, "Absolutely."

"It looks as though his chief competition is from Ross Nebulan of Illinois."

"Well, yes, Mr. Nebulan is a worthy candidate, but he hasn't got what Andy has."

"Delegate votes? A campaign war chest? A private pollster? A luxury yacht?"

"No," replied Mrs. Chalk coyly. "I mean a charming and gracious wife." She smiled.

"Oh, I suspect Mrs. Nebulan will have a comment about that. We're anxious to talk to Mr. Chalk. Where is he now?"

"He's back at our suite in the hotel. He continues to campaign, you know. That's his commitment to the race. In fact, he's probably with a voter right now."

He certainly was. Back in his hotel suite, away from
cameras and reporters, candidate Chalk was eagerly
chasing a pretty woman delegate around the coffee table.
No one else was in the room, and the woman, wearing a hat
with "Louisiana" in letters around the brim, laughed
heartily as Chalk tried to catch her. She teased, "You can
have my vote if you can catch me," and then ran into the
bedroom. Chalk galloped after her, saying, "Never let it be
said that I didn't run for the nomination."

Chester Mega, as anchor, was the glue that held all the
reports from the convention floor together. After Hank
completed his interview with Mrs. Chalk, the camera shot
returned to Chester Mega, who responded, "Thanks, Hank
and Mrs. Chalk. We'll be seeing more of her during the
convention. A little background about the schedule for this
first day of the first Ameriminds convention. The chairman
has called the convention to order. Though it still seems
like 'disorder' out there, that's just typical convention mode.
There will be an invocation, followed by the presentation of
the colors, followed by the national anthem and the Pledge
of Allegiance. There will be welcoming remarks, followed
by the national anthem, followed by the presentation of the
credentials committee report and amendments, followed by
the national anthem. Then there will be a vote on the
credentials committee report, followed by the national
anthem, the Pledge of Allegiance by children of Baptist
members of the National Guard, the Pledge of Allegiance
in sign language, the Pledge of Allegiance by a group of
culturally diverse insurance agents, the national anthem by
bell ringers from an American casino, discussion of the
rules committee report, the national anthem, and a rendition
of 'Onward Christian Soldiers' by a group of dentists who

have bonded with their patients. All of that is followed by the national anthem, the nomination of the permanent chair by the rules committee chair, the vote on the permanent chair, the national anthem, the resolution for approval of temporary officers, the national anthem, the Pledge of Allegiance recited by a group of performing clog dancers, the resolution for appointment of committees on resolutions, the motion to dispense with the reading of the names selected for committees, the keynote speech, the Pledge of Allegiance by North Carolina hot-tub owners, the national anthem sung by Oklahoma cheerleaders, the Pledge of Allegiance by old and cranky businessmen, and the benediction. And that's all just the first day." Chester sighed. "Now don't go switching the channel to the mini-series about mud-wrestling. We may have some of that here, too. Let's go to reporter Bella Wing. Bella, who do you have there?"

"Chester," replied Bella, "I'm standing here with Mandy. Just one-name Mandy." The camera focused upon a man with a shaved head, mostly bare-chested, dressed in a leather vest and a pair of military-camouflage trousers, with rings in his nose, ears, and belly-button. He was sitting on the floor with his legs folded beneath him.

Bella explained, "Mandy is the politically ambivalent, charismatic, multimillion-dollar dietary supplements business promoter who speaks in tongues, operates a giant nudist colony, plays lead guitar for the hard-rock group 'Abandoned Mice' and leads the yuppie group called Generation X-Crement. Mandy, what do you think of the convention so far?" Bella leaned down to extend the microphone to him.

Mandy uttered a one-word response. "Tablets."

Bella continued, "What's your opinion of the proposed party platform?"

"Tablets."

"What would you prefer to promote within the party?"

"Tablets."

"And if the party refuses to bend to your requests?"

"Tablets."

"Will the action be physical or verbal?"

"Tablets."

"And will this violence be here at the convention?"

"Tablets."

"Until your demands are met?"

"Tablets."

"Well, you heard it, Chester," stated Bella, turning her face to the camera. "Sounds like this is going to be a 'hot' convention."

"Great job of interpretative reporting," Chester replied.

Bella nodded confidently, answering, "Well, I was a communications major. I can read body language, too."

"Let me pose a few questions for Mr. Mandy that I'll ask you to relay, Bella," Chester said, clearing his throat.

So, Bella then repeated the questions coming through her earplug from Chester in the anchor booth. "Mandy, Chester Mega would like to know what kind of relief you use for headaches?"

"Tablets."

"Also, Chester would like to know what you used when you were in elementary school and practicing penmanship?"

"Tablets."

"Chester would like to ask what you remember most about the Ten Commandments?"

"Tablets."

Bella continued, "One last question from Chester in our anchor booth. He knows your company sells dietary supplements, like herbal tablets, and he was wondering if there is anything that you'd be willing to give away for free as a promotional effort?"

Mandy paused, then replied succinctly, "No."

"Well," commented Chester. "Those answers seem pretty mainstream to me."

"Mainstream may have a different meaning from right here and right now," Bella responded, as she looked beyond Mandy and moved to get out of the way. "You see, Mandy is sitting cross-legged smack-dab in the middle of the aisle and here comes the Georgia delegation, back from a caucus meeting."

Mandy, with wide-eyed surprise, suddenly straightened, but, with his legs interlocked, he desperately wrestled to untangle them in order to escape the oncoming rush. "Why the hell didn't you tell me..."

Mandy's words were abruptly squelched as he disappeared beneath the trampling horde of Georgians.

One of the people at the end of the Georgia crowd was the young man in the buttoned raincoat. The young man, hunched and clenching the raincoat tightly closed at the neck, stepped over a crumpled Mandy. Watching the interview segment on a TV set in the security headquarters room, security agent Harry Hooper jumped out of his chair at the sight of the young man in the raincoat who continued to aggravate Hooper's suspicions. Hooper pointed to the TV set, "There...there...that's the guy! The one in the raincoat!" Putting on his suit coat, Hooper hurried to the door, saying to himself, "In the area of the Georgia section. Here I come."

Bella helped a dazed Mandy, with a shoe impression

across his forehead, to his feet. "Tablets," he kept saying over and over.

Bella explained, "Those Georgia delegates were hell-bent-for-leather. And Mandy is wearing leather. Back to you, Chester."

"What a scene," Chester said, shaking his head in amazement. "We need to go back to the floor to the Illinois delegation where Saphira Pitchfork is interviewing Ross and Reva Nebulan. Saphira."

"Yes, Chester..." The news reporter stopped, because the crowd was loudly singing the national anthem. The candidate and his wife were singing, too. "...It's quite patriotic and loud here...Just a moment, as we get through the rockets' red glare..." When the anthem had ended, Saphira announced, "Ross and Reva Nebulan are with me. Dr. Nebulan is one of the leading candidates. A poll, conducted by UGH News and Cyberspace Diapers, just out today shows that Dr. Nebulan is slightly behind Andrew Chalk, 43 percent to 41 percent, with candidates Joyce Hyphen Martindale and Josh Deaver in single digits, trailing substantially. Dr. Nebulan, what do you think of that poll?"

"Saphira," responded Nebulan, "I'm a great believer in the margin of error. I just think it is too close to call. I intend to be the Ameriminds presidential nominee."

"First let me ask Mrs. Nebulan what she thinks about the convention?"

Smiling, Reva Nebulan pushed her husband aside and took the microphone. "I think Ross will win handily. People here know that the whole future of the nation is at stake. And they know that Ross has something which Mr. Chalk doesn't."

"And what's that?" Saphira asked, taking back the microphone.

Leaning toward the microphone, Mrs. Nebulan emphatically answered, "A charming and gracious wife."

"Dr. Nebulan, tell us a little something about yourself. You hold a doctorate. That's why you have the 'doctor' title."

"Yes, I have a Ph.D. in Chiropractic Methodology and Spinal Relations. That allows me to conduct physicals and to address medical issues. I'm just an ordinary middle-class American. It is only by accident that I have the biggest house in our suburb. I have struggled just like everyone else. I know what it is like to live for two weeks when the washing machine is broken down and the laundry is stacking up. I know what it is like to work hard for the American dream; there's not a winter that goes by in Illinois when I don't have to shovel the snow from our driveway just to get the limo out of the garage and to get to the office. Sometimes the chauffeur and the grounds keeper help me. I know what it's like for people struggling to feed their families. Just the other day, I told my wife to forget about buying Girl Scout cookies and the Christmas cheese tray for this year. Not until the economy gets better. So, I know what it's like. I've been there. And I think the people understand that. God bless them."

Saphira asked, "If you had to describe America as a product, what would it be and why?"

Nebulan pondered the question for moment, saying, "That's a good question," which is always a handy response to make a reporter feel good about asking a question, even if the question is goofy.

"Not a salad with light dressing. Not liver and onions, which some people would find great and some people wouldn't. Not a glass of champagne, as that's too bubbly," said Nebulan, looking toward the ceiling in thought. "Well, I can think of America as a pie. Yes, that's it. A pie. And someone owns the ingredients that go into making the pie. Someone sells the pie for a profit. Someone can buy and eat the whole pie. Someone can afford a slice or two of the pie. Someone might share a piece of the pie. Someone can only afford a sliver of the pie. Someone would like just a taste of the pie, but don't even get a crumb." Nebulan nodded, feeling satisfied about his response to a question he'd never practiced answering before from campaign staff members in their mock question-and-answer sessions. "Yes, America is like a pie."

"What is your vision for the future?" Saphira asked.

Nebulan was quick to answer. "I can tell you that in one word...Prisons."

"Prisons?" Saphira frowned.

"Yes, prisons. The key to our economic well-being. Prisons, and lots of them. As I envision America, one-fourth of the population will be employed by prisons to look after another one-fourth that's serving time inside. And then the nation's other two-fourths, which equals nearly one-half, will work in service areas, fulfilling the needs of both the prison staff and the prison population. It's an industry with a future. And I want to be a part of it."

"Which one-fourth do you hope to be in?" Saphira questioned with sarcasm.

Nebulan's pot-belly shook as he laughed. "Of course, I want to be an architect of the economic plan. It will lead us to the forefront of economic stability, and to the cutting edge of prison science. That's the vision I have for this great country."

"When was the last time you had your eyes checked?"

Saphira asked soberly.

Nebulan roared with laughter. "You're funnier than the Congress. If I have a post for Secretary of Humor in my Cabinet, I'll let you know."

Saphira changed the subject. "Has this been a negative campaign with a large amount of dirt thrown from both ways?"

Nebulan scowled. "I don't think you could characterize our campaign as negative or dirty. I do wish Mr. Chalk would choose to stay on the high ground, however. It's been frustrating as someone who believes that America deserves better."

Saphira thumbed through her notes. "Didn't you accuse Mr. Chalk of trying to scare the elderly?"

Nebulan answered, "Well, he accused me of trying to scare children, mothers, and church choirs."

Saphira: "Didn't you accuse him of being an agnostic, disliking football, and belching during church services."

Nebulan: "He said I opposed Social Security, wanted a constitutional amendment limiting the number of people in unemployment lines, and supported cocktails at 2 p.m."

Saphira: "But you said he hated peanut butter, puppies and patriotic songs."

Nebulan: "After he said I believed in mandatory nose drops."

Saphira: "You said he was as dumb as a box of rocks."

Nebulan: "Only because he said I was lower than whale... (he looked at his wife and cleared his throat) ...whale manure."

Saphira: "Back to you, Chester."

Chester shook his head and scratched his chin. "You know, they've spent millions of dollars getting their messages out." He shrugged. "When I get rude and obnoxious, I just do it for free."

Chester cocked his head and adjusted the small radio transmitter in his left ear, listening to a voice from the production room. "I guess...Yes, we have Trixie Spaniel down on the convention floor with Mrs. Chalk. Go ahead, Trixie."

The reporter had caught up with the candidate's wife in the Nevada delegation. The young man in the raincoat walked casually by them. "Mrs. Chalk, would you care to respond to Mrs. Nebulan's response to your earlier remark? She just told UGH News that she is charming and gracious, implying that you aren't. Would you care to address that?"

An annoyed Cassie Chalk replied, "I'm too charming and gracious to bluntly reply to that lie."

Trixie tried to qualify the response. "Are you calling Mrs. Nebulan a liar?"

"I'm too charming and gracious to bluntly call someone a liar, even if she is one," Mrs. Chalk declared unapologetic.

Trixie continued, "We've yet to see your husband here. Some people are saying that he is putting the finishing touches on an acceptance speech that he expects to give. Is that true?"

"I believe he's back at the hotel, maintaining open lines of communication with delegates. He continues to campaign. In fact, I think he's with a voter right now."

Mrs. Chalk was correct. Her husband, Andrew Chalk, was back at the hotel suite, naked and sitting in bed, with a pillow propped against his back and the bedding pulled to his waist. He was busily scribbling on a note pad, as a grinning woman, also naked, except for a convention hat, was resting beside him in the bed.

Candidate Chalk said, looking at the woman, "And I'll be sure to thank North Dakota for its generous votes." The woman smiled with approval.

CHAPTER 2:
The Age of Technology (The Revenge of Frankenstein's Monster)

All of the camera monitors within the convention hall were in use by the security force as part of a dragnet search for the young man in the raincoat. The cameras covered almost every nook and cranny of the convention hall, even the restrooms, relaying each location scene to more than 1,000 TV screens on all four walls at security headquarters.

Despite all the privately televised coverage, the young man in the raincoat amazingly continued to elude apprehension. He unpredictably slipped from camera view to camera view in almost ghostly style. So far, the security force had failed to anticipate his moves.

Inside the security headquarters, "raincoat" spotters were employed to call out when they sighted him on the screens.

"He's in the Nebraska section, screen 85," called one spotter. "He's moved to the Florida section, screen 175," shouted another. "He's at the taco stand, screen 754," another spotter reported. Moments later, another spotter said, "He went inside stall 4 of the women's restroom, screen 963." The young man in the raincoat maintained a hasty fugitive's pace.

The other security guards looked up to the hard-as-nails Harry Hooper with reverence. He'd spent the last two hours interrogating the entire Georgia delegation, grilling them on an individual basis. He had the energy and the skills to get a brutal job done.

Though Hooper hadn't yet cracked the mysterious case of the young man in the raincoat, he had gotten assorted leads from the Georgia delegation. One delegate thought he'd seen the young man in the raincoat in a convention stairway. Another said he thought he'd seen the man eating a hamburger and fries in the Oregon section. Another delegate said he thought the raincoat served as the young man's warped symbol for Armageddon.

The Georgia delegates "spilled their guts" to get away from Harry's interrogations. What's more, through the interrogation process where Harry played both "good cop" and "bad cop" intermittently, he obtained a variety of confessions: Eight Georgians admitted to going over the speed limit, three said they'd cheating on their taxes, two said they'd shoplifted once, one confessed to fishing without a license, one said he didn't know how to change a tire on his car, one confessed to fishing without a license, and one said he had lustful thoughts about chickens.

The security force was impressed with Hooper's pure iron will in making people break. They didn't know that, as part of his interrogative method, he ate an entire clove of garlic before conducting the close face-to-face cross-examinations. It made even the toughest Georgian wilt.

Hooper obtained more startling information from Mandy, the weird leader of Generation X-Crement, who'd been trampled by Georgians, but still had some foggy recollections of the young man in the raincoat, the last guy to jump over the fallen Mandy. In searching for clues, Hooper asked, "As the young man in the raincoat jumped over you, did you see anything distinctive about the clothes he was wearing under the raincoat?" Mandy said that in his fallen condition, he was semi-conscious, but, as he looked up, he believed that he saw a gun--a large revolver. He believed that the young man was carrying a gun, which was concealed by the raincoat. Mandy couldn't account for anything more, not colors or clothing style or anything else. But he thought he saw a gun.

Hooper and the security force, perceiving a grave danger, became more anxious than ever to apprehend the young man in the raincoat. Not willing to panic the convention delegates, the security force observed a discreet, in-house security alert concerning the suspect. They were to apprehend him first and ask questions later. Hooper kept a garlic clove ready.

As they had planned, Charla Willow and her cameraman Joey met back at the make-shift set of their tabloid TV show "Sensations" in one of the many convention hall hospitality rooms to prepare for the next camera shoot. Each of them was accompanied by a curious delegate, who they had rounded up for the TV segment.

Joey had found Bluebell, a gum-chewing stripper from New Jersey, who held onto Joey's muscular arm like glue. He had been instantly attracted to her, and she was captivated by his smile, good looks and beefcake physique.

"This is Miss Bluebell, and she works in the entertainment business in New Jersey," Joey boasted.

"We're shooting a tabloid story, not a triple-X movie," Charla whispered to Joey, before introducing the delegate she had located. Charla's delegate was a cowboy--tall, lean and with a boyish face, reddened by wind burn. He wore a cowboy hat, a red flannel shirt, blue jeans, and cowboy boots.

"Where'd you get him?" Joey whispered back to Charla. "Central casting for the next spaghetti western."

Charla batted her eyelashes with disapproval. "Please meet Boyd Larkspur from Wyoming."

"Ah...Actually, I'm from Montana," Boyd replied bashfully.

"Montana, Wyoming. Same difference," Charla said, leading Boyd to a couch where he sat down. Charla then dislodged Bluebell from Joey's arm and guided her onto the couch, next to Boyd. They looked at each other, with some puzzlement, and Boyd blushed uncomfortably.

"I said I would do it with you," Bluebell said, flirting with Joey. Then she seriously gave Boyd the once-over with her eyes. "But it'll cost extra for him. Though he is cute."

Joey smirked, as Charla took charge. "I don't know what Joey has told you, but we'll give each of you 15 minutes of fame at one hundred dollars a minute."

Bluebell's eyes bulged, and she readily accepted. "Sign me up. What do I have to do?"

Boyd's puzzled look remained. "I thought you said you wanted a love story for TV?"

"Yes, that's the main idea," Charla continued, "Maybe you've seen our TV show 'Sensations'? It's on cable, late night mostly."

"Is that the one that the crazy preacher in Alabama is trying to get off the air?" Bluebell wondered.

"No, he wants the national news off the air," Charla clarified. "We're independent of anything that's balanced or objective. And all we want you both to do is play this little game for the loyal fans. Just pretend that you discovered each other here at the convention and have developed a sudden love interest."

Bluebell looked again at Boyd and then bluntly replied, "Six-hundred per minute." Charla, with surprise followed immediately by contempt, gave an irritated look at Joey, who gulped and hurriedly sat down on the arm of the couch next to Bluebell.

"Bluebell, baby," he pampered, "After we're done with the shoot, remember that you and I will head to that little bed and breakfast inn where you get all the sausages you can eat for a dollar."

Bluebell grinned pleasingly, took Joey's arm and snuggled against him. "Okay, let's do it."

All three looked at Boyd, who was starting to shake his head. "I ain't never even seen this lady before tonight. I don't think it would be very proper."

Bluebell motioned to Charla. "Go ahead. Offer to go to the bed and breakfast inn with him."

Appalled, Charla took a step backward. "I will not!" she exclaimed. Stomping to the other side of the couch near Boyd, Charla spoke directly to him. "It's just a little pretending, nothing serious. It's just TV. You know, like the beer commercials. Like the soaps. Like Congress. It doesn't mean anything, but ratings. And this is an important week in our nation's history."

"You mean with the convention and all?" Boyd responded.

"No, I mean sweeps week," Charla explained.

Boyd scratched his chin, still confused. "You said you wanted a love story. That's why I volunteered. I have..."

Charla interrupted, "That's what this will be. A cute and warm love story. This is an opportunity for all your friends back in Wyoming to see you on TV."

Boyd corrected, "I'm from Montana. But I got some friends in Wyoming, too."

"All your family and friends will get to see you on their TV screens. And you'll even earn a little money. Maybe you can buy that...that...pony you always wanted," Charla said.

Joey strutted to the camera and adjusted it so that Bluebell and Boyd were framed together on the couch.

Charla backed away from the couch, describing what she wanted. "All you both have to do is just sit on the couch. For the take, we'll just have you sitting there on the couch. We'll do the voice-overs, so you just visit with each other about the weather or anything."

"I know," Bluebell coaxed excitedly, "I'll ask you about the weather in Wyoming!" Boyd stared with bafflement at Bluebell.

"Yes, yes, the weather," Charla replied. "And then in the second session, which will air on the following day, all you have to do is reach over and give Bluebell just a little peck on the cheek." Bluebell grinned.

"You mean, kiss her? On national TV?" Boyd asked nervously.

"Yes, just pretend Miss Bluebell is your horse, or something," said Charla.

"I don't kiss my horse. It ain't sanitary. That's only in the movies," Boyd declared defiantly, as he started to get up.

"Okay, okay, why don't I talk to you about it later, Boyd," Charla concluded. "Here's a little something for your time." Charla handed Boyd a sealed envelope with an enclosed check. At first, he gallantly declined the offer, saying he hadn't done anything. She insisted, however, pushing it into his shirt pocket, saying, "It's not much." The cowboy nodded gratefully, tipped his hat, and left the hospitality room. While Bluebell waited on the couch, Charla walked over to Joey and whispered, "Did you get them on film?"

"Yes," Joey answered, "But not 15 minutes worth. We'll have to do some editing of the tape for length."

Charla nodded. "Can we get some computer graphic

enhancement? So it looks like he leaned over and kissed her?"

"Remember the film we had of George Washington meeting with Abraham Lincoln at that gas station near Gettysburg?"

"You mean that was faked?"

Joey corrected, saying that the word "faked" was too harsh. "It was computer-enhanced. If you have the technology, why not use it? Actually, George didn't even know Abraham. I think they lived in different states."

Charla was impressed. "So, you can computer-enhance our scene with Boyd and Miss Bluebell?"

"No problem," Joey replied. "I think I'll even take that flannel shirt right off Boyd's chest."

Charla nodded with approval.

"After all," Joey stated, "This is the age of technology."

CHAPTER 3:
Oil, vinegar, Christianity, and right-wind

News teams were dispatched to a disturbance in the South Carolina section on the convention floor.

A group was shouting boldly, performing religious chants, and trying to interrupt a convention speech that condemned the death penalty.

"Condemn the wicked, not the death penalty!" exclaimed the Rev. Dirge, the leader of the radical conservative Christian group known as the "Roaring Lions." Dirge had lost an eye in one religious crusade and wore an eye-patch. He lost a tooth in another crusade. The Rev. Dirge loved to tell and re-tell the stories of how he'd lost his eye and then poked a "sinner" in the eye in retaliation and how he'd lost a tooth, and then placed the tiny gold cross that hung from his neck between his knuckles and smashed another "sinner" in the mouth, knocking out a tooth. "An eye for an eye, and a tooth for a tooth," was his favorite Biblical quote.

Reporter Trixie Spaniel and her camera crew were first on the scene for UGH News.

"Rev. Dirge, what's the reason for this vocal vigil?" Trixie shouted to be heard as the "Roaring Lions" began their traditional protest of roaring like lions.

The Rev. Dirge roared loudly and then pulled Trixie's microphone closer, saying, "We roar to be heard."

Trixie pulled the microphone back for a question, "It sounds like you're roaring so others can't be heard. Why is the Roaring Lions Christian group supportive of the death penalty?"

"An eye for an eye and a tooth for a tooth," replied Dirge. "A time to heal and a time to kill. The Good Book says it."

Trixie continued, "You take lots of your scripture from the Old Testament. Why not the New Testament, which is more compassionate in its advice about treating others?"

"Because the Old Testament is the original message, and the New Testament was a sequel. And we all know that sequels aren't as good as originals," explained Dirge.

The Roaring Lions started to disrespectfully shout names, "Heathens!", "Pagans!" and "Unitarians!"

"We are against sin. And some sinners are more sinful than others. And we all know that. That's why I can be proud and arrogant and it's still the thief who goes to jail. The Roaring Lions congregation has assembled this list of 100 sinful sins, from slight to abomination to absolutely evil, and this list is based upon factual Biblical interpretations. People can purchase a copy of the list from us for a mere $5.50 plus handling. No tax, as we are a non-profit religious organization with a multi-media communications center, a TV network, a theme park, a chain of book publishing companies, and our organization serves as a major stock-holder in several private prison enterprises."

Trixie asked, "Do you have a church?"

"Not really a church building per se," Dirge added. "It's just too expense for our budget."

Trixie continued, "Rev. Dirge, don't you have a habit of turning messages around? For instance, the use of the name 'Roaring Lions.' The ancient Romans enjoyed the sport of having lions kill Christians."

"The cross was a death instrument in Biblical times and now we pay homage to it. That's why we Roaring Lions also wear these chains with little pewter electric chairs. It is a symbol of our belief in 'sin be gone.' Sin be fried. And we sell these necklaces for $15.95. No tax, as we are a non-profit religious organization. We are lions, hear us roar. This roar is going to blanket this nation and send the wildebeests of sin scurrying to either redemption or the electric chair. It's their choice."

"Candidate Josh Deaver has criticized your group and the other major candidates' embrace of the death penalty. Will he be successful in stopping the first nationally-televised electric chair execution of a criminal, scheduled for 9 a.m. tomorrow?"

"Eight o'clock Eastern time," Dirge added. "No, he will not stop it. It is God's will. And the will of the people of the great state of Texas with its massive prison system where the execution will take place. Mr. Deaver is a minor candidate and will stay a minor candidate with family values like that."

The Roaring Lions began to roar again.

Dirge continued, "A big screen TV, shipped in from one of the big football stadiums and set up near the podium, will be used tomorrow to bring the execution live to the delegates in the convention hall. Isn't that wonderful? After all, this is the age of technology."

Trixie questioned, "Isn't the Roaring Lion group really a ring-wing political action group and fund-raising business?"

"Our business is the selling of God, and we've got the franchise," declared Dirge. "Politics and religion are inseparable. Education and religion are inseparable. That's why we believe in prayer in public school buses and baptisms in physical education classes. And we prefer to think of ourselves as 'right-wind' rather than 'right-wing.' We are a right wind, blowing in the right direction, to the right, strongly across the nation. And the leaves of sin will be stripped from the branches."

Trixie sent the broadcast back to Chester Mega in the anchor booth, who promptly relayed it to reporter Mike Troy.

"This is Mike Troy reporting. I have with me candidate Josh Deaver of Missouri, the liberal candidate who is against the death penalty. Mr. Deaver, could you give us your jaded opinion of tomorrow's televised execution of convicted killer James Cash Cathcart?"

Deaver nodded and replied, "Mr. Cathcart's guilt has always been in question and we are hoping that..."

Chester Mega broke in and the camera shot returned to Mega. "We've got to take a short break for local station identification. But we will be right back with more coverage of the Ameriminds convention. Stay tuned."

Following a few seconds of station break time, Chester responded, "If you've just joined us, I hope to remind you all that UGH News will be covering this first Ameriminds convention from start to finish, despite the ratings. Tonight's keynote address will bring this first day of convention activities to a close. Right now, let's return to reporter Mike Troy and candidate Josh Deaver."

The telecast returned into the middle of Deaver's statement. "...It's been difficult for me to get my message of opposition to the death penalty out to the public. The sound bites..."

The broadcast cut to anchorman Chester. "We need to take a few commercial breaks. It's time to pay the bills. We'll be right back."

FIRST COMMERCIAL: A sweet, young woman was softly humming as she applied Make-Me-Happy Roll-on Deodorant to her underarms. Then she danced around the room, whispering, "Make-Me-Happy sure makes me happy. And it makes Ted happy, too. And Pete, Harvey, Winston, Conrad, and Frank." She blew a kiss, sensuously saying, "And how about you?"

SECOND COMMERCIAL: Two men were standing side by side at a bus stop. The man on the right was a typical businessman, with a dark suit, flashy tie, polished shoes and a worried expression. In one hand, he held the handle of a brief case. Over an arm, a wrinkled overcoat hung. The younger man on the left, dressed in shiny black leather, chewed nonchalantly on bubble gum, frequently running a comb through his stiff, greasy hair.

"Pardon my intrusion, mister. But do you have a Lessen Insurance Company policy?"

The businessman curiously eyed the stranger.

A little, old lady slowly waddled to the other side of the businessman to also wait for the bus. She softly commented, "Yes. A Lessen Insurance policy is great."

The businessman didn't utter a word. He smiled at the little, old lady.

The younger man, popping his gum, replied, "Right on. A Lessen Insurance policy protects you from fire loss, flood damage, blind dates from hell and many other problems, not to mention theft loss." At that point, the stranger pulled a revolver from his pocket and said, "You really should get a policy."

As the businessman nervously displayed his billfold, the little, old lady swung her handbag, knocking the gun from the assailant's hand, and then grabbed his arm and flipped him judo-style. The would-be robber landed with a thud on the sidewalk. The little, old lady, dusting off her aged hands, then turned to the businessman.

"A Lessen Insurance policy also pays for costly hospital bills because of an accident, like that punk's unfortunate fall."

The broadcast returned to the convention coverage. "We're back," Chester said cheerily. "Before we're accused of being gender-biased, we need to go down to Hank Midland, who is with candidate Joyce Hyphen Martindale of Texas."

"Too late, Chester," replied Hank. "We've already been accused of being gender-biased by Ms. Martindale, the only declared female candidate in this race."

"That's Hyphen Martindale to you, buster. Now give me that microphone, you...you...man," the woman candidate said, grabbing it from Hank's grasp. "It's about time that someone besides a male got some attention at this convention. Women of today are not about to take the same abuse that our foremothers endured."

As Hank tried to regain control of the microphone, Hyphen Martindale swung the microphone at him a couple of times, saying "Stay back, stay back."

"How do you intend to draw the male vote if you continue to bash them?" Hank asked, though his voice was barely audible.

Hyphen Martindale bellowed into the microphone, "I am confident the women will orchestrate a united front. If the old 'sleep on the couch' demand doesn't work, then maybe men can be persuaded to vote for me or face reparations. Yes, we women deserve reparations for thousands of years of male domination and downright unmitigated gall. The payment is due from all males. And for those deadbeat males who don't pay, they should get a good look at the male in the electric chair tomorrow."

"You are in favor of the death penalty then?"

"For men I am. Men are the biggest abusers of women in the world today and there's a certain element of equality in the concept of male punishment, wouldn't you say?"

Hank declined to comment.

"Of course, you men wouldn't say. You can't stand to think that your domination is coming to an end. We women will not only overcome--we will lead, conquer and disembowel." Hank cringed. And the woman candidate continued with fiery language, "The sisterhood is going to demand a new kind of thinking. We want more women in corporate offices, more women in Congress, more women in the military, more women in space and more women in pro football. We want higher pay; equal pay just means we've settled for the same when our diversity is better than that. We're going to give the male dictionary a good lesson in the fine art of revision, changing words like 'mankind' and 'manual' to 'womankind' and 'womanual.' Person-kind doesn't cut it, because we want our turn with the next 2,000 years--it is only fair turn-around."

"How about 'womanhole cover'? Or 'womanure'?" Hank said from the background.

"How would you like to be slapped with a dirty diaper? Did you know you are taking the job of a qualified female reporter? Aren't you ashamed? What about that old male geezer at the anchor desk? That old..."

Chester interrupted the broadcast from Hyphen Martindale, saying, "For a person who doesn't believe in domination, she sure dominated that conversation." In the meantime, Hank wrestled Hyphen Martindale for the trophy of the microphone, while she was jabbing him with it. The young man in the raincoat stopped briefly to watch their struggle.

Chester explained, "We had to break in to bring you the keynote address. At the speaker's platform is Jerald Dipper, who is welcoming the delegates to the convention. Mr. Dipper is one of the first members of the new Ameriminds Party. He is a new New, New, New, New, New Democrat, which really means he is an old Republican. He is 55 years of age and is from New Hampshire. He's been active in politics, business, and scandals for about 10 years. He's divorced, has two children, plays the harmonica, and wears foot deodorizers. His hobbies are pole vaulting and creative lying. And--since we provide the background with warts and all--he has a wart on his left hand. And now let's go down to the platform for the rest of his keynote speech."

The keynote speaker took off his wire-rimmed glasses, concluding, "...And let's choose a great team." He turned from the speaker's stand and walked away as a sprinkling of applause came from the delegates.

The camera came back to Chester. "Sorry, I guess I'll have to cut my biographical introductions short. We have a team of analysts, however, who will give you a re-cap of the highlights of that speech." Sitting next to Chester were two dull-looking news analysts; one of them yawned.

Chester continued, "Here are Herman Merdell, UGH News, politics and waste-water bureau, Washington, and Frank Fink, UGH News, special assignment commentator, Bird Dog, Utah. Gentlemen, what was wrong with that keynote address?"

Fink: "Too short."

Merdell: "Well, Chester, it was supposed to set the mood for the entire convention. I would agree to a degree that it was too short. However, if it had been both short and dramatic, that would have been a rallying cry, or if it had been longer and yet addressed the issues that would have set the agenda for the convention. Instead it provided neither excitement nor direction. I can't think of a single phrase from the speech that could go into the lead paragraph of tomorrow's news story."

Fink: "It was too short."

Merdell: "The problem wasn't a result of the words rather the problem was with the message. The message tends to get convoluted when the tone is lugubriously soaked with adjectives. What did it actually say? It was too broad, too calculated, too perfunctory."

Fink: "And too short."

Chester: "What about the speaker? Anything wrong with him?"

Fink: "He's too short."

Merdell: "It's not all that apparent to me if he really does represent the political center of this party. From his speech, I got the impression that he is cautiously looking for acceptance but failing to deliver in his own way. I'm not sure if that's an armada approach or a lifeboat approach, but I know that this ocean of social endeavor is going to be pretty stormy."

Fink: "He's too short. He's so short he'd have to stand on a stool to look under the bed."

Chester: "Thanks, gentlemen. You've been very informative."

Chester looked directly at the camera and smiled. "Well, there you have it. The first day of history in the making at this first Ameriminds Party convention. Join us tomorrow for continuing convention coverage, more interviews with the candidates and delegates, and a televised execution. This is Chester Mega for the entire UGH News team. Have a great evening."

CHAPTER 4:
The Execution

Boyd Larkspur, the Montana cowboy, was sitting on the floor, head bowed, eyes closed, with his back against the door of the hospitality room, patiently waiting as Charla Willow walked up the hallway.

Charla was well aware that critics charged her with taking "indecent liberties with a TV program." She preferred to call it "artistic liberties." Last night's show was no different.

Charla knew that she'd doctored and altered and stretched the sensational, the dramatic, and the poignant. She knew she was in the entertainment business and she knew how to tease and lure in order to get and keep a loyal audience.

Still, she was surprised to see Boyd Larkspur waiting for her. She knew he wouldn't be pleased with the segment, but usually when people weren't pleased, they either allowed the money from the tabloid show to heal their pain or sent their attorneys.

Charla decided to turn on the charm and act as though nothing was wrong. "Good morning, Boyd," she greeted, as he scrambled to his feet, "That segment last night was just terrific. People all over the country are saying how impressed they were by you and Miss Bluebell." She quickly unlocked the door and trotted inside the hospitality room with Boyd loping a few steps behind.

"I...I need to talk to you about that," Boyd said soberly.

"What can I do for you? Oh, did you know that Miss Bluebell is really happy about the program?"

"I didn't even know you were taping it. I didn't know the camera was running."

Charla excused the tactic, saying, "We do that to get a natural look. And a natural conversation."

"But you didn't even use my real voice. Somebody else's voice was used, and the voice said things I didn't say. And it didn't even match the way I was moving my mouth."

Charla hastened to the subject of the money. "Did you find the check inside that envelope I gave you?"

Boyd offered the envelope back to her. "I can't take this. It's not right. I didn't agree to meet with you for the money. I thought you wanted a love story?"

"We did," Charla said confidently, "And that's what we got. And it's partly thanks to you." She held up her hands, refusing to take the envelope. "No. That's yours. It's the least we can do for you since you did so much for all of us, and the TV viewers. How did they like it back in

Wyoming?"

"You mean, Montana? Well, I did get some calls, and they wondered what I was up to. You see, they know me and they know that I'm a pretty straight arrow when it comes to love," he said, continuing to frown.

"What didn't you like about it?" Charla said, quickly regretting that she'd asked that, allowing an opening for criticism.

"The whole thing. It's not the truth. Not one part of it," he replied.

"Is that all?" Charla shrugged with smile. "I thought it was something serious."

"This is serious. This is my life. My love life, at that. My love life is a sacred thing. How would you like someone making up stories about your love life?"

"The supermarket tabloids do it all the time. It's called exposure. Sometimes I even help them. I get my picture published and everyone knows you can't believe what you read in Hollywood," she replied.

"Well, that may be the way it is in Hollywood. But that's not the way it is in Montana. And not here in Kansas, either. And I suspect that's not the way it is in a lot of places where people sit down in their living rooms to watch TV," Boyd lectured sincerely.

"You're being too hard on yourself," she said, skirting around the subject. "This may launch a whole new career for you."

"There were other things wrong with it, too. The stuff that you reported was wrong. I'd never met Miss Bluebell before, let alone had a romantic interest in her. And I certainly didn't reach over and kiss her. For a minute, I thought it looked like Abraham Lincoln was kissing Miss Bluebell and I wasn't even there. Then it was me again, sitting there on the couch with her. I think you used some trick photography with that one."

"That brought tears to the eyes of many viewers," Charla explained.

"And what happened to my shirt? I was wearing a shirt. And that chest wasn't even mine. Too muscular and too hairy."

"But it sure was sexy!" Charla said with a snicker. "The women back home will be anxious for your return."

"That's not what I wanted. That wasn't part of our deal, when you approached me and told me you wanted to do a love story."

"If you were confused by what I said, I accept your apology," Charla replied. "I understand how mistakes can happen."

Boyd paused and scratched his head.

Charla took an obvious look at her wrist watch. "Would you look what time it is. Wonderful morning for an execution, isn't it? Are you going to watch it? I can't believe my people didn't get to Mr. Cathcart first about his public execution. We would have paid big money for that."

"I need you to make a retraction," Boyd responded.

"This execution is a big deal. But, by far, Boyd Larkspur, the love story segment with you and Miss Bluebell was the number-one romance of this convention. It captured the hearts of a whole nation. You can be proud of that."

"I want you to make a retraction," he urged.

"Oh," Charla shook her head with disdain, "We can't retract something. It's bad for the ratings. It's bad for the credibility, you know. If we retract something for you, we might have to do it for others."

"I need you to make a correction, so my girlfriend Rosie will understand," Boyd pleaded.

"Oh, I see," Charla replied, nodding. "I didn't realize you had a girlfriend. But here's what you can do. Just take the money back to her when you get home and tell her you did it for her."

"That would be lying. Besides..."

"Look at the time," Charla gathered a notebook and some papers, and told Boyd that she'd have to go to the convention hall to watch the televised public execution over the giant television screen.

"But I..."

"I'll talk to you later," she interrupted, though she didn't intend to talk to him again.

Boyd sighed, dishearteningly. He stared at her momentarily, as she busily ignored him. Finally, he flipped the envelope with the check onto the desk in front of her. She looked up at him and he replied, before leaving the room, "You know, a cowpie isn't a pie, even if it's hidden under meringue."

Charla gave a perplexed look and jammed the notebook and papers into a satchel. She took a mirror out of the desk drawer and applied a coat of lipstick. When she slightly angled the mirror, she saw in it the reflection of the young man in the raincoat who was standing at the door.

"Yes," she said startled, "Can I help you?"

The young man in the raincoat smiled. Mostly, his eyes smiled. Charla was proud of her ability to control situations, but this time she melted, almost like a shy school-girl in the presence of her prom date. To Charla, his expression seemed mysterious and seductive.

"I like your show," he said with a voice that was deep and suave.

And before she could answer "thank you," he was gone. She hurried to the door and looked down the hall, both ways. A group of Nebraskan football players were throwing and catching a football, two Kentucky women delegates were escorting a man in a chicken suit, and a Colorado delegate was carrying a pair of skis. However, the young man in the raincoat had vanished.

Out on the convention floor, the UGH News team was busy with morning interviews.

Reporter Bella Wing was with Gerard Goss, the chairman of the National Rights-for-Kleptomaniacs campaign. Goss, an admitted kleptomaniac, believed that this was the decade for kleptomaniacs' rights.

"Look," Goss explained, "There's been women's rights, gay rights, victims' rights, smokers' rights, animal rights, vegetarians' rights, hunters' rights, alien rights, furniture rights, tree rights, dolphin rights, overdue book readers' rights, and Frank Lloyd rights. And one group has been consistently and repeatedly left out. Kleptomaniacs."

"Is kleptomania an illness, a crime, an orientation, or a lifestyle?" Bella asked.

Goss was adamant. "Oh, my goodness. A lifestyle, of course, and complicated by lots of other factors. In other words, it is more than just a lifestyle choice. It is partly an illness, like alcoholism, and partly genetic, like big feet, and partly environmental, like expecting rain to fall from clouds. Is it a crime to drink alcohol, to have big feet, or when it rains? Certainly not. What's more, we live in a society that stresses 'having things' as an important way of life. That kind of societal pressure is the cornerstone to our cultural diversity as kleptomaniacs."

Bella nodded with interest. "So, what kind of rights are you expecting to have for your interest group?"

"We're just asking for the same treatment that other

groups get. Isn't that fair? Isn't that what equality is all about?" Goss said rhetorically. "We want to be able to practice our lifestyle without persecution and discrimination."

"Wouldn't that mean people would have to let others steal?"

Goss explained, "Only if they are actual, clinically diagnosed kleptomaniacs. Or can show that they have led a long history of it. And we don't call it 'stealing.' That's an ugly word that flames the fires of intolerance. We call it 'observance of our conduct'."

Bella replied sincerely, "Thank you for the insights, Mr. Goss. I will try to be more understanding the next time the neighbor in my apartment complex sneaks to my door mat and takes my morning newspaper."

"If you have a piece of paper, I'll give you the hotline number for Kleptomaniacs."

"Well, I had a notebook here a minute ago," Bella said looking around. "And my purse? I thought I had my purse with me? Back to you, Chester."

"Hold on to the microphone, Bella, or that may end up missing, too," cautioned Chester from the anchor booth. He took a sip of coffee and looked at his watch. "It's nearing 9 o'clock, the time for a most historical event for television. And I'm not talking about a mini-series, either. The execution of James Cash Cathcart will be televised live from his Texas penitentiary, where he has been on death row for seven long years. This is the first time for a publicly televised electric chair execution and a parental guidance warning will be given ahead of this telecast. Children under the age of 17 should watch this execution only in the presence of an adult. This event will be shown nationwide and, for those people who are faithful soap opera viewers, do not worry. The soaps will be shown in their entirety immediately following. For convention participants, the telecast will be displayed on the giant 3-D TV screen which is located next to the speaker's podium. And that 3-D screen is top-of-line, cutting-edge technology, designed by a conglomerate of multimedia corporations that owns a sizable percentage of the information highway, several pay-for-view channels, and most of the Amazon rainforest."

Chester looked out the window of his anchor booth and down at the convention floor. "A full crowd has gathered in the convention. Millions of TV viewers across the nation are expected to watch, and it is expected to draw a bigger viewing audience than the Super Bowl or reruns of 'Melrose Place.' That's why advertisers are taking advantage of the audience size. Following this commercial break, there will be a pre-recorded special background report by UGH News reporter Mike Troy about the Cathcart case. We'll be right back."

FIRST COMMERCIAL: It was the car salesman at Ted's Global Automotive City. "Howdy, folks. Enjoying the convention? Speaking of politics, here is a little model especially for the politically minded. Comes with an enlarged bumper so that all of your bumper stickers can fit perfectly. Sturdy little thing, rock-proof windows, and comes in thrown-tomato red. Also, this baby is really fast, which is a condition every politician looks for in a car. And notice all the options inside. A car phone, a fax machine, and a handy-dandy paper shredder. And folks, we have free balloons for the kiddies. So, stop by Ted's Global Automotive City, where foreign trade takes on new meaning." The car salesman gently petted the car. "And remember, this car has a 20-mile guarantee."

SECOND COMMERCIAL: A sweet, young girl was softly humming as she applied Make-Me-Happy Roll-on Deodorant to her underarms. Then she danced around the room, singing, "Make-Me-Happy sure makes me happy. And it makes Carlton happy, too. And Clark, Benjamin, Oscar, Doyle, and Peter." She blew a kiss, sensuously saying, "And how about you?"

THIRD COMMERCIAL: A talk show host provided a short preview of an upcoming program. "Can people live into their golden years without eating creamed corn? Most prisoners on death row never ate creamed corn and look what's happened to them. How about you? A surprising study by a Nebraska sociologist, a shocking message for all consumers, and an alarming conclusion that is certain to make you think differently about corn. Join me, Calamity Jane McLaine, on 'Talk Until We Drop' this Tuesday on your local station. Prisoners, consumers and creamed corn. Don't miss it."

FOURTH COMMERCIAL: A breeze in a meadow combed the tall grass, shaping it into a surging tide, forcing dried dandelions to shake their white heads and spill the seeds gracefully into the summer air. At the end of the meadow was an old weeping willow tree, straight and strong, the rough bark tightened by age, the yellow branches limply swaying. The breeze rustled the leaves and grew stronger until it is a wind that pushed the submissive weeping willow branches out of its beautiful shape. The boughs whipped the sky. Some leaves were ripped from the branches, stolen. A single leaf flew through the air, through an open window and landed near a plate of pancakes. Slowly, silently, appeared the words, "Buy Sherry's

Pancake Mix."

Following the commercials, the pre-recorded news report by UGH News reporter Mike Troy aired, with Mike standing in front of a penitentiary in a drizzling rain. "This is where it is supposed to happen. This will be where the story ends. This is a story about crime, justice, and, of course, politics. James Cash Cathcart was convicted of the murder of his girlfriend in a small Texas town one spring morning many years ago. (The video shows Cathcart, with a coat draped over his head, being escorted by attorneys and police officers into a courthouse. This same shot is shown three times, to fill video time, as Mike tells the story.) Apparently, Cathcart and his girlfriend went to the courthouse to get a marriage license. According to Cathcart, while his girlfriend was in the restroom, he was hit over the head near a water fountain, knocked unconscious as someone then pulled his body into a nearby broom closet. (The video shows a broom closet.) The broom closet was also the place where his girlfriend's body was found, draped across his. (The video shows a portrait of the girlfriend with a name identifier below.) Police believed that they struggled and, when he killed her with a weapon, her body fell into his arms, making him lose his balance and fall against a shelf of toilet tissue. The police say that was the reason for his bump on the head and being unconscious there, too, and on the floor beneath her. (The video shows more repeated scenes of Cathcart walking into the courthouse with a coat draped over his head.) Cathcart has said to this day that he is innocent and was framed. The details are sketchy and some of the witnesses who testified at the trial have since recanted on their story, leaving some doubt about Cathcart's actual guilt. (The video shows

Cathcart smiling briefly as his attorney says something to him.) The other troubling factor in this case was the trial itself and what the judge allowed or disallowed as evidence. The judge allowed the jury to hear about the Cathcart's fingerprints on the murder weapon, but he didn't allow the presentation of the weapon as an exhibit. The weapon was, of all things, a gavel. (The video shows reporter Mike Troy in a courtroom, displaying a gavel.) The judge allowed information about traces of hair found at the scene which matched Cathcart's hair, but not about a torn piece of black clothing, thought to have come from a robe of some kind. The judge allowed testimony that a witness saw Cathcart drinking water at the water fountain, but not the rest of the story about Cathcart's girlfriend arguing with a former boyfriend. (The video shows repeated scenes of Cathcart walking into the courthouse with the coat draped over his head.) However, the conviction was upheld in Texas, and the U.S. Supreme Court, busy with a case about a sperm donor's battle for child visitation rights, denied cert which means it didn't hear the case, letting the lower court verdict stand. (The video shows graffiti on a wall.) With citizens reeling from crime statistics and angered by neighborhood graffiti, the case hit a state and national nerve. Politicians came out of the woodwork, saying they would get tough on crime. Some people opposed the death penalty, most notably Ameriminds presidential candidate Josh Deaver, who repeated said he couldn't get his message out to the public."

(The video shows a short clip of candidate Deaver, saying, "Well, I believe it is wrong to..." Deaver's statement was cut off in mid-sentence).

"However, most police officers, government officials, and politicians, including the other major candidates of the

Ameriminds Party, endorse the death penalty," Mike Troy continued.

At this point, the video tape presented some quick statements from the other candidates. Andrew Chalk said to the camera, "How can anyone be against the death penalty when they hear about that evil mass murderer in New York City who savagely massacred 10 innocent bystanders."

Joyce Hyphen Martindale said to the camera, "Another woman dies at the hands of a man. It is an outrage and we have to answer this with action." Ross Nebulan said to the camera, "How can anyone be against the death penalty when they hear about that evil mass murderer in New York City savagely massacred 20 innocent bystanders."

Reporter Mike Troy continued, "The governor, in a tight campaign re-election race where crime is a major issue, continues to present a profile of a leader who's tough on criminals. He isn't expected to stop the execution at the last moment. Besides, he already has been talking with a Hollywood movie company about what actor will play him in the made-for-TV version. So, the nation seeks its revenge upon criminals, and a lonely, tired man, whose last meal included a piece of his mother's apple pie, will take a short walk this morning to a death chamber."

On cue for UGH News, the giant 3-D TV screen in convention hall became illuminated with a televised picture. The convention hall lights dimmed in response, and the bright screen lit the faces of the delegates and other spectators. The darkness was filled with a splattering of applause, some loud "roaring" by members of the Roaring Lions Christian group who had been busy selling chain necklaces with tiny pewter electric chairs, and assorted jeers and cheers. Some delegates waved miniature American flags. Some delegates wore special 3-D glasses.

Behind the large screen, having taken refuge from patrolling security guards, was the young man in the raincoat, his own back against the back-side of the screen. The darkness gave him the quality of a silhouette, and he began to make slow, puppet-like movements with his arms, strutted and slowly danced as he imagined that the huge audience on the other side of the screen was watching him. His performance was almost ballet, almost Tae-kwon-do. He moved in elegant slow motion, reaching and swaying, and responding to the changing noise levels of the crowd.

Down on the convention floor, most of the people were staring upward at the screen, talking with friends, jeering, laughing and offering toasts to the event that was about to occur. Candidate Josh Deaver, who opposed the death penalty, shook his head and then bowed it and buried his eyes into his hands. Some people were crying; some were praying. However, the crowd was mostly festive, and the noise reached a crescendo as the convention band provided a drum-roll.

Behind the screen, the young man in the raincoat knew what the drum-roll indicated. He held his hands high and shook them like tambourines. Then he bowed. Then bowed a second time, and a third. And when the drum-roll ended, the entire convention hall was suddenly silent.

It was a strange and eerie silence, as the young man in the raincoat raised slowly from his bow, confused by the silence, listening for something, anything. But the moment of silence lasted, uncomfortably. It was as though the convention hall was suddenly vacant. It was as though the celebration mood had been wiped away in one quick sweep.

The young man in the raincoat crept softly like a cat to a point where he could peek around the edge of the screen.

From the vantage point, he looked down upon a mass of still faces lit ghostly by the flickering light from the screen. No one uttered a word. No one moved. The faces--most wearing 3-D glasses--were unexpectedly solemn, fixed upon the screen. The people stood frozen in place, lifeless, like park statues in a night rain of glare and neon. The young man in the raincoat drew back behind the screen, feeling safer as he hid.

Then, just as instantaneously, the lights of the convention hall came on as the telecast faded and the screen became black, empty of pictures. The emptiness of the screen seemed to transfer itself to the public memory. The convention band struck up a jazzy version of "When the Saints Come Marching In," and the music sparked and lathered most of the crowd into a new and happier mood of cheers and singing. People waved small American flags.

The UGH News team was strategically positioned and ready for sound bites from candidates and a cross-section of the delegates.

The statements from respondents were presented in quick succession.

A Kansas delegate dressed like a sunflower, with large yellow pedals around her neckline: "Crime doesn't pay."

A Texan in a ten-gallon western hat: "It ought to be done more often, if you ask me."

Party Chairman Sydney Paine: "We need to make our streets safer. We need to be able to take the garbage out to the alley again and reclaim our alleys."

Candidate Joyce Hyphen Martindale: "It was a strong message to men and I hope they get it. I was so proud of my state's governor. In the closing hours, it was only up to him as to whether that man lived or died. And my state's governor stood tough."

A New Hampshire delegate with a sign advocating "National Centrist Day": "When it's a choice between no death penalty for prisoners and the death penalty for all prisoners, the middle ground is the appropriate place. In fact, with all issues, it is always better to take a moderate stand, a more central position. I think that's what Americans want."

A Florida delegate carrying an inflated, toy alligator: "It works for us in Florida."

The Rev. Dirge of the Roaring Lions: "An eye for an eye and a tooth for a tooth."

A Californian still wearing a pair of the 3-D glasses: "That was some TV show. I can't wait for the sequel. The whole world should be looking through these rose-colored 3-D glasses."

A New York delegate with a sign "Gambling by TV, too": "I don't think the guy should have gotten a fancy last meal, either."

A Maryland delegate in a tuxedo: "After all, there is no Santa Claus."

A delegate in a Santa Claus suit: "Naughty or nice. It's up to you."

Candidate Ross Nebulan: "How can anyone be against the death penalty when they hear about that evil mass murderer in New York City who savagely massacred 30 innocent bystanders."

Reva Nebulan, the candidate's wife: "I feel safer already."

A Delaware delegate carrying a pizza: "I didn't like watching it. Why do they have to show those things? It's enough to ruin an appetite."

A janitor with a broom: "If they gave the electric chair for littering and general sloppiness, most of the people at this convention would have to take a seat."

A delegate dressed like a vampire: "There are so many weird people around today that it makes me wonder what the world is coming to."

Mandy of Generation X-Crement: "Tablets."

A North Dakota delegate in bib overalls: "We don't have crime where I come from. It's against the law."

Cassie Chalk, wife of candidate Andrew Chalk: "I felt so good that I even left my car unlocked today. I know if my husband were here, he'd wonder why anyone can be against the death penalty when they hear about that evil mass murderer in New York City who savagely massacred 40 innocent bystanders. My husband isn't here right now. He's back at the hotel with a voter."

Andrew Chalk was back at the hotel with a voter, all right. A giggling brunette and he, kissing and wrapped in each other's arms, romantically frolicked on a couch in his hotel suite. During the romp, the woman's straw hat with the state designation "Washington" fell off and rolled on its brim across the floor, beyond the TV set, which was tuned to a western movie with the gunfight scene.

Back at the convention hall, reporter Saphira Pitchfork was on camera, speaking to viewers. "We've heard a lot about some evil mass murderer in New York City who was said to have killed a lot of bystanders. We've heard that story over and over from people in support of the death penalty. It seems to be a talking point. So, we did some research and have found that the story is an urban legend. It's totally false, as no one would be so evil as to kill that many people. Not in America. It would be a horrible nightmare, if it ever did happen. In this case, the story got all twisted up concerning the facts. It wasn't a mass murderer. It was a mass communicator. It wasn't 'killing bystanders.' It was 'butchering the English language.' And, well, then all the rest of the story got worse."

Chester Mega responded back at the anchor booth. "Great investigative job there, Saphira. We at UGH News believe in setting the record straight. Okay, let's go down to the convention floor to Bella Wing who has some late-breaking news. Bella?"

Then on camera, reporter Bella Wing nodded and announced a late-breaking news bulletin.

"Candidate Josh Deaver has left the convention floor. Repeat. Candidate Josh Deaver has left the convention floor after saying that he will make a major announcement about his campaign tomorrow during a convention speech. We have learned from a source of a source of a source of a source inside the Deaver camp that Deaver plans to withdraw from the race."

Chester Mega broke in from the anchor booth, "Bella, Mr. Deaver looked somewhat pale and didn't even use the 3-D glasses during the televised execution of James Cash Carthcart. With candidate Deaver's opposition to the death penalty in contrast to the main party line, was that a factor in his decision?"

Bella replied, "It may have contributed. He has long stated that he's been disappointed and frustrated in his efforts to get his message out about issues. Here's a short clip that we got with Candidate Deaver just minutes ago."

The UGH News segment showed Deaver encircled by questioning reporters, including Bella. In one quick, tightly-edited clip, the only audible part of Deaver's statement to reporters was, "...the..."

Bella, back on camera, said, "He went on to say this about the death penalty."

In another quick, tightly-edited clip, Deaver's response was reduced to, "...was..."

Bella, back on camera, continued to explain the results of the taped session with Deaver, "Then he had this to say about his whole campaign."

In another quick clip, Deaver was shown, saying, "...wasn't..."

Bella, back on camera, continued, "About the political process, he had this to say."

In another clip, Deaver's response was sliced to two words, "...scalp itch..."

Bella was back on camera. "I think we can assume from all of this that Deaver sees his chances for the Ameriminds presidential nomination as pretty slim. Since his campaign has been stalled by lack of money to fund campaign advertising and he has remained as a minor candidate from the left fringe of the party, it's no surprise that he will drop out of the race and release all of his committed delegates. Candidate Deaver hopes to raise some of the issues in his speech tomorrow, but it is his announcement of withdrawing from the race and how it will affect the other candidates here at the convention that will be the main topic of discussion. Back to you, Chester."

Chester soberly shook his head and replied, "Let's go now to our two election analysts: Herman Merdell, UGH News, politics and wastewater, Washington Bureau; and Frank Fink, UGH News special assignment commentator, Bird Dog, Utah." The two men were sitting at Chester's right at the anchor desk. "Gentlemen, what does this mean?"

Merdell, looking pensive, scratched his chin. Fink yawned.

Chester attempted to lead them. "Josh Deaver, as a candidate, didn't have a chance to win this nomination. The figures just didn't add up. His delegate support remained in the single digits. But they are a dedicated single-digit group and, if they leave Deaver upon his request, they could throw a victory to either of the leading contenders, Ross Nebulan or Andrew Chalk."

Merdell responded, waving his pen as if to make a point, "That's right."

Fink nodded.

Chester prodded eagerly, "How about the chances of Joyce Hyphen Martindale? Could this bolster her campaign out of the single digits?"

Merdell was doubtful. "I just don't think so. She'd have to bake cookies or something before anyone else would join her campaign, and she doesn't have the personality for it. She's good with speeches, fund-raising, phonathons, and negative-campaigning, but she's bad, bad, bad with cookies. And at this time of the campaign season, when people are getting tired of all the campaigning, cookies could bring in the uncommitted vote."

Fink nodded.

Chester thanked them for the insights, and, as the camera zoomed in on him, continued sternly, "Josh Deaver's withdrawal is not the only controversy going on at this convention. In fact, there's a bigger one brewing. A much bigger one that has split families and their values. Let's go to Hank Midland, who is with Milton Pippin, the leader of the national gooseberry boycott."

Hank Midland added to Chester's remarks. "Yes, Chester, controversy has carved out a place in the history of this convention, and it's thanks largely to the gooseberry." Hank moved closer to a middle-aged man with a berry-sour expression. "This is Milton Pippin, from Oregon, and he's the leader of the national gooseberry boycott. Mr. Pippin, what's the reason for this boycott campaign?"

"Hank, the people just can't take it anymore. The price of gooseberry jam is outrageously high and it's time that the manufacturers get a wake-up call. You might say we want to put the gooseberry jam manufacturers in a jam," Pippin laughed, slapping the reporter on the back, knocking him forward into the lens of the camera. "That's a pun, son!"

Hank regained his composure, rubbing his nose where he'd hit the camera. "As you can see, Chester, this issue is prone to violence and has caused a great deal of torment among candidates who would just as soon eat gooseberries as have to deal with the controversy of them. Back to you, Chester."

"Well, isn't that the berries," replied Chester. "Now a word from another sponsor."

COMMERCIAL: A grocer dusted around some jars of jam. He then looked up, uttering, "Pintyler's Gooseberry Jam is delicious. The jam is made from the finest berries and the finest geese, and only the finest." Suddenly, the checkers, stockers, and carry-outs burst into a song and a dance routine. The melody of the song was catchy and simple. The words were predictable. "Gooseberry jam. Gooseberry jam. Pintyler's Gooseberry Jam is, oh! so damn good." Then the individual store workers each sang a verse:

"Spread it on bread."
"Spread it on meats."
"Spread it on crackers."
"Spread it on treats."
"Spread it while you're walkin'."
"Spread it while you're skippin'."
"Spread it while you're sittin'."
"Even spread it on Milton Pippin."

Then the store workers joined with voices in joyful song for a dynamic finale while romping down the store aisles. "But spread it around. Spread it around. Pintyler's Gooseberry Jam is just like a rumor. So, spread it around."

CHAPTER 5:
The Chase Scene

Charla Willow and her cameraman, Joey, lugging heavy video equipment, hurried through the busy lobby of the convention hall. They were headed to the next taping session for their tabloid news show, snaking their way through the crowd of delegates, reporters, and convention staff.

A delegate from West Virginia had agreed to talk on camera about how he started making whale lawn ornaments from beer cans after he witnessed a vision of "Moby Dick" in a dark, dusty coal mine.

Charla knew how she'd spice up the story. Employing Joey's expertise with computer graphics and enhancement techniques, one whale ornament would be increased to the size of a house. On camera, when the delegate was explaining how he transforms the beer cans, a "voice-over" would tell a dramatic, heart-wrenching story about a near tragedy involving the giant whale sculpture. Charla's storyline would describe a time when the delegate got pinned beneath the giant ornament and, using a broomstick like a harpoon, and, with a sudden adrenaline surge of super-human strength, he was able to free himself. Charla shook her head, thinking positively. No, she'd change the adrenaline reference to testosterone. Charla knew every segment needed some kind of sexual angle to attract a larger audience.

As Charla and Joey passed a collection of potted plants, they glanced toward a small, three-foot-tall, green-headed alien creature with three antennae and a pleasant expression, who was standing beside a leafy banana plant. An American flag was attached to one antenna.

Charla and Joey took a few more steps, stopped, looked at each other, smiled and then shook their heads. "No way!" they replied in unison, and they continued to the elevator area where entrance doors led to several stairways and corridors flanked by meeting rooms.

Running around them suddenly was the young man in the raincoat, who stopped briefly at a stairway door to smile charmingly at Charla and then resumed his sprint. Not too far behind him was Harry Hooper, the security officer, who paused near the elevators to ask hastily, "Which way did he go? The young man in the raincoat. Which way did he go?"

Joey was ready to point the direction, when Charla grabbed his arm, tucking it tightly against her waist, and pointed in the opposite direction.

After Hooper quickly exited through a hallway door, Joey asked, "What was that all about?"

"A mystery that could lead to something big," Charla whispered with a dreamy look in her eyes.

"For our show?"

"Oh, well, maybe that, too," Charla answered, coming back to reality.

This time, security officers were everywhere. The young man in the raincoat darted around two of them, as one officer made an unsuccessful tackle attempt.

"He's heading down stairway 6B," radioed one officer.

"He's on the main floor, hallway 4D," radioed another officer.

"He just ran through the lobby again," radioed another officer.

"He's in the kitchen and just stole a newly-baked lemon meringue pie," radioed another officer, who was joined in the pursuit by a chef angrily waving a spatula.

The young man breezed onto the convention floor, followed by Hooper, the chef, and a platoon of both uniformed and plainclothes security officers, reminiscent of a Keystone Cops chase. A shocked delegate from Mississippi pointed feverishly at the onrushing young man in the raincoat and shouted in terror, "Look out! He's got a pie!"

Nearby politicians and delegates uttered whoops and screams, as they stampeded away from the young man in the raincoat, opening a channel for him to run through.

Juggling the pie, the young man in the raincoat leaped over chairs and around terrified delegates. Hooper was right behind, reaching desperately forward to try to catch the fugitive. The chef was waving the spatula and security police officers were pushing people out of the way in order to keep up.

In the meantime, UGH News anchorman Chester Mega interrupted reporter Trixie Spaniel's interview with candidate Ross Nebulan on the convention floor.

"Trixie," called Chester, looking out the anchor booth window, "There seems to be a skirmish of some kind headed your way. Do you see anything there?"

Trixie replied negatively, and she continued her interview with Nebulan. "What would you say to people who think politics is a circus, filled with clowns?"

Nebulan grimaced and replied, "Politics is serious business. Look at my face. Is this the face of someone that belongs in a circus?"

Hooper was finally close enough to grab the collar of the young man in the raincoat, who stumbled forward with Hooper, releasing the lemon meringue pie. The pie flew through the air, above the ducking heads of delegates, and hit Nebulan squarely in the face, splattering lemon and meringue all over the politician and onto nearby Mrs. Nebulan and reporter Trixie Spaniel.

Hooper wrestled on the floor with the young man in the raincoat as the chef and the security officers, en masse, jumped onto them. The huge pile of twisting and punching body parts touched off surrounding hostilities. A Virginian pushed a Rhode Islander. A South Carolinian, yelling, "The South will rise again," slugged a frowning Vermonter. An Arizonan, trying to pull a security officer off the pile, was sucker-punched by an irritated New Yorker. A Coloradan barreled into a Wyomingite for being called a "Greenie." In seconds, the entire area of convention floor erupted into a riot.

The young man in the raincoat, unscathed by the turmoil, crawled out of the pile on all fours, with a more crumpled Hooper close behind him.

Seeing that the young man in the raincoat was getting away, Hooper demanded, "I order you to stop," and pulled from inside his coat what he thought was a revolver, though it was actually the chef's spatula. The young man in the raincoat vanished within the fighting crowd, and Hooper disgustedly threw down the spatula.

The scrambling security officers were forced to re-direct their efforts to crowd control, which seemed to be an impossible task as the fighting escalated.

The young man in the raincoat zigzagged through the crowd, with the determined Hooper trailing, bobbing occasionally to see the fugitive's route.

The young man in the raincoat plunged into a stairwell, colliding with lanky Montana cowboy Boyd Larkspur. They bounced together against the wall, maintaining a stance, with Boyd taking most of the blunt of the impact. "Sorry. Gotta run," the young man in the raincoat replied, pushing himself away from the wall and taking several steps at a time up the stairs.

Dazed, Boyd staggered forward, looking up the stairway, when Hooper plunged through the door, also colliding with the cowboy. This time, Boyd went sprawling against the wall by himself, hitting his head and hearing "cuckoo" sounds as he fell unconscious on the floor. Hooper didn't have time for pleasantries. He propped Boyd's limp body in a sitting position, with Boyd's back against the wall and head bowed. Then Hooper bellowed, in John Wayne fashion, "I'll be back for you, pilgrim."

Several flights up, the young man in the raincoat hurried down the hallway which led to the row of anchor booths that overlooked the convention floor. He raced into one anchor booth, interrupting a telecast of an anchorwoman giving the news, and he realized he was somewhat trapped.

Hooper was soon at the entrance and the only way out of the anchor room was either straight down to the convention floor, a fall that would likely kill him, or several feet through the air to another anchor booth. From the window of one anchor booth, the young man in the raincoat jumped toward the next anchor booth, breaking through the glass and landing near Chester Mega at the UGH News anchor desk.

Chester came unglued, shouting "Holy crap!" and dived out of his chair for cover behind the desk.

The young man in the raincoat hurried to the other side of the small room, opened the window, and saw a long, thick communications cord hanging from the ceiling to the floor. Hooper had successfully made the jump into the UGH News anchor booth, so the young man in the raincoat leaped and caught the cord. The force of his body caused the cord to swing loose and outward.

The young man in the raincoat swung downward, across the convention hall and into the giant TV screen, catching the top edge of the screen and clinging precariously to it as his body dangled against the screen.

The fearless Hooper, swinging on another cord, similarly hit the screen, several feet to the side of the young man in the raincoat, and struggled to hold on to the top edge, his body also dangling, his feet kicking wildly. The added force of Hooper's impact caused the screen to creak loudly and shake, and then it began to sway.

People on the convention floor below looked in horror at the giant screen, teetering uncontrollably as the two men held onto it tightly.

"It's going to fall!" yelled a delegate. "Look out!" shouted another delegate. The people immediately below the screen pushed the crowd back in sudden panic, trying to get out of the way as the screen tipped and collapsed forward, delivering the two men with it into a massive heap over chairs and tables.

The push by the crowd steadily toppled the delegates one by one as they fell against others. A wave of fallen delegates rushed through the New York section, through the Pennsylvania section, through the Ohio and Indiana sections, steadily rolling. The wave crested with the Midwest sections and continued through the western sections, finally hitting the California and Hawaii sections.

Candidate Ross Nebulan, wiping the pie off his face, thought he had secured a safe position on the edge of the convention hall. However, frozen with terror, he stared horrified at the rapidly approaching tide of falling delegates, politicians, party hacks, security officers, and members of the convention band, including several tuba players.

Before they careened into him, knocking him down and sweeping him away, he held up his arms and shouted, in a tone of fearful finality, "The Domino Theory!"

CHAPTER 6
The Dream Segment

Boyd Larkspur, unconscious in the stairwell, started to drift to a far-away place. A place far, far away from the Ameriminds convention in Kansas.

It was a world of simplicity. A world of black and white, actually more sepia, where clarity and crispness projected bold, artistic images against a soft background of big sky and plains rolling into mountains.

A world of no clashing colors, arguing to be seen above all the rest--no reds, whites, or blues of politics; no greens of big business greenbacks or environmental activists; no purples, reds or yellows of ribbons in tribute or mourning; no earth-tones of kitchen refrigerators.

A world of solitude and quiet, where the chirping of birds floated from the billowy, leafy trees. No carping of politicians, no radio talk shows, no drunken car-racing crowds.

A world without balloons and 3-D goggles.

A world of few issues. Just a man and his horse and love. The love of a good woman, that is.

His favorite quarterhorse was there, by his side. With its

big, gentle eyes.

Boyd turned to the horse, petting its nose. "I don't think we're in Kansas anymore, Toto."

Toto whinnied. Then, the horse startled Boyd when it spoke in plain English, "It's not Montana, either."

Boyd scratched his head. "I guess not. Montana doesn't have talking horses."

Toto continued, "Montana isn't without the heartache of politics, either."

"Heartache" reminded Boyd of his lovely Rosie, the girl of his dreams. Since this was a dream, he asked, "Where is Rosie? Is she here?"

Toto neighed.

"Does that mean 'no'?" asked Boyd.

"A 'neigh' is not a 'no' unless it is a 'nay' as in a roll-call vote," explained Toto.

"Rosie is the glue that holds my whole life together," Boyd forlornly confessed.

Toto whinnied. "Did you have to mention the G-word? Why do you think you and I ran away and met the traveling spin-doctor, got caught in the snow blizzard, and then hung out with a brainless bureaucrat, a heartless politician, and a cowardly incumbent, all looking for the great corporate multi-media god to solve our problems?"

"You mean," Boyd replied sympathetically. "Because of mucilage?"

Toto nodded.

"I can live without mucilage. I can live without TV, politics, and even problems. But I can't live without love," moaned Boyd.

In the distance, near the horizon, Boyd suddenly spotted his girlfriend Rosie, grinning and waving excitedly, motioning to him.

"Rosie!" called Boyd, nearly in tears, "We'll come for you."

Toto shook his mangy mane. "Not on this back, you won't."

Boyd started to run, jumping through the wind-blown field of wheat. He ran toward Rosie, who wore a wedding gown and held a bouquet of black- and white-colored roses. Probably reds and pinks if it had been in color.

Suddenly, there was change.

Suddenly, the wheat field became vibrantly colorful, streaked wildly with bright colors. Boyd broke his stride and came to a stop when Rosie vanished from his sight.

Suddenly, he was naked with only a pencil.

Suddenly, he was naked with only a pencil, and Charla Willow and cameraman Joey were there with a video camera.

Suddenly, he was clothed in a loincloth, because he had family values, and the tabloid news team was filming him with a camera that started to act as a powerful vacuum cleaner. It sucked in colors and landscape and chirping birds.

Suddenly, his body was pulled across colorful floor tiles by the vacuuming video camera and one of his legs was sucked up into the camera. The special effects were really unusual and award-winning.

Suddenly, the young man in the raincoat was pulling on one of Boyd's arms, as Boyd was sucked to his waist inside the camera.

Suddenly, Hooper the security officer was pulling on Boyd's arm, as Boyd was sucked to his chest inside the camera.

"No, no, no," called Boyd. "There's no place like reality. There's no place like reality..."

Boyd woke in the stairwell, where he'd collapsed. His fuzzy vision cleared. On their knees beside him were Charla Willow, who held his left hand, and Joey the cameraman. Hooper stood over Boyd, looking down with steely eyes that contained a rare glimmer of concern.

"I think he's okay, now," Charla replied. "He's a tough Wyoming cowboy."

"I'm from Montana," Boyd groaned, rubbing the bump on his head. Then Boyd excitedly explained, "I had this dream. And Toto my horse was there." Boyd pointed to Charla, then Joey, and then Hooper. "And you were in it, and you, and you."

Charla and Joey smiled. Hooper said, "Maybe we need to call an ambulance."

Boyd pointed beyond them, toward the stairway. "And you were in it, too," Boyd said.

Hooper turned, following the angle of Boyd's pointing finger, to see the young man in the raincoat, perched on the stairway, peeking at them.

"It's him!" Hooper yelled.

The young man in the raincoat quickly ran up the stairs, as Hooper resumed the chase.

Chapter 7
The Folk Hero

Anchorman Chester Mega dusted more pieces of glass from his hair. "There's glass everywhere in here. We've cautioned our guests to be sure to wear shoes." The large hole in a window pane in the anchor booth, where the young man in the raincoat had busted through, was secured by an X-shape of duct tape.

"For those of you who have just tuned in, I can tell you for a fact that chaos hit this convention today. Wild, unimaginable chaos. Chaos of the worst kind," decried Chester. "A giant 3-D TV screen is now in shambles as a testimony to what happened. And all we can wonder is, why? Why? Why?"

A quick replay showed the young man in the raincoat crashing into the anchor booth and leaving it as abruptly, followed by Hooper.

"Who these people are remains a mystery at this time. We aren't certain of the 'who' part, though we believe--yes, I am getting confirmation by our college intern "gofer" off camera
--that the second man was part of the convention security force. We don't have the 'why' or 'how much' parts. But here's what we do know. We know the 'what,' 'when,' 'where' and 'how.' And to bring this colossal disruption to you in perspective is our own special military expert, General Punch Rottweiler. General, what can you tell us?"

Tucked tightly in his uniform, the burly, scowling general, who barked his remarks through bulldog-like jowls, used a pointer to explain symbols and arrow designations on a large map of the convention hall.

"Chester, we believe it started here, in the main lobby," the general stated with authority, "And it escalated to the actually convention floor." He poked the pointer at that area, creating a hole in the map. "Then the young man in the raincoat made this approach through the crowd and was flanked in the rear by a pursuing force of best damned fighters this convention can muster."

The general continued, "Then the assault went upstairs, the entrance to the stairway being designated by this small oil well graphic. You can see the anchor booths of all of the nearby news networks designated by these dog-biscuit icons. At this dog-biscuit--our UGH News anchor booth-- the young man in the raincoat retreated, cut off from the rear by a security officer who's part of the best damned fighting force this convention can muster. This dollar-sign designation marks the spot of the giant 3-D TV screen, where the skirmish took on major consequences. And the rest is history. Until it's revised." The general saluted the camera.

"Thanks, General Punch Rottweiler, for that inspirational and strategic debriefing," Chester said. "And speaking of inspirational and strategic, we need to take a pause for these commercials."

FIRST COMMERCIAL: "We're come to this supermarket parking lot to do a commercial with a typically average shopper. And here's a typically average shopper, now. Excuse me, sir?" the ad pitchman in a sparkling plaid suit said.

"Me?" replied a plain, dehydrated man carrying a bag of dried dog food.

"No, the pink elephant beside you," the announcer retorted. "Of course, you."

"Hey, you must be one of them advertising guys with the T and V camera and the silly questions."

"Right you are, and for being right, you get to be in a real, live commercial."

"On T and V?!"

"Yes. On tele and vision," replied the glib announcer. "Answer the next question absolutely correct and you will win a prize. Are you ready, sir?"

"Okay."

"Mr. Typically Average Shopper, how many letters are

there in the word 'only'? Ten seconds."

The fidgety, little man crossed his eyes in thought.

"Twenty seconds," responded the salesman, realizing the customer may need more time.

"Oh, my!" The shopper's voice quivered. He repeated the word by syllables. Then the announcer unwrapped a box of clothes detergent with the word 'ONLY' printed on it in large, red letters. The shopper counted the letters on the box, replying, "Four?"

"You're right! Absolutely correct!" exclaimed the announcer, jubilantly waving the box. "Naturally, we are here today representing Only Clothing Detergent. Only is the Only. And now, sir, you have won our grand prize, which is," the announcer hesitated to build the excitement as the shopper bubbled with joy. "A year's supply of dirty clothes!"

The shopper gulped, but he remained polite.

"And here is your first month's supply!" Two women in bikinis pushed a shopping cart into the picture.

"Iris will really be surprised," the shopper said, smiling at the women.

"But wait, there's more!" proclaimed the announcer, tearing open a large envelope. "Here, with further compliments from Only Clothing Detergent, is a 25-cent coupon good toward the purchase of any king-sized box of Only Clothing Detergent. Can you believe it, Mr. Typically Average Shopper?!"

"Gee whiz. And I only came here for a bag of dog food," the shopper said, shifting the bag to the other arm. "And I don't even have a dog."

The camera movedin for a close-up. At first, it focused too close, delivering a picture of the announcer's nose. The adjustment was automatic, focusing on his entire face.

"And remember, Only is the Only!"

SECOND COMMERCIAL: A sweet, young girl was softly humming as she applied Make-Me-Happy Roll-on Deodorant to her underarms. Then she danced around the room, singing, "Make-Me-Happy sure makes me happy. And it makes Barton happy, too. And Joe. And Scott, Mitchell, Royce, and Jose." She blew a kiss, sensuously saying, "And how about you?"

THIRD COMMERCIAL: A talk show host provided a short preview of an upcoming program. "Tubas. Can they be deadly? The music plays and the death toll rises. Find out how you can protect your family. Join me, Calamity Jane McLaine, on 'Talk Until We Drop' this Wednesday on your local channel. Tubas and sour notes. Don't miss it."

Chester was back on the air from the UGH News anchor booth at the Ameriminds convention.

Chester smiled. Chester was like a father figure, and viewers felt comfortable when he smiled. "During the break, the most amazing twist of fate happened. And it is typical of the power of the media and especially TV. It is also typical of the speed of change. One minute, you can be a fugitive. And the next minute, you can be a folk hero. I am talking about the mysterious young man in the raincoat, the one that led convention security officers on a long and chaotic chase through this convention hall. That's right. The convention is buzzing about the rebel, the man with no name, the phantom in the raincoat who stares authority in the face and runs. We go now to reporter Saphira Pitchfork and a group of delegates who have formed a fan club for the young man in the raincoat."

Saphira Pitchfork was standing with a group, mostly women, who squealed and waved when they realized the camera was filming them.

Saphira explained, "This is the newly organized Raincoat Club." The group squealed excitedly again. "And this is not only a fan club, but also a blossoming business." Saphira held up a T-shirt with a cartoon picture of a super-hero-type character in a raincoat and accompanying words, "Let It Reign!" Saphira continued, "Here's one of the souvenirs that they are selling. There are also buttons, hats, ties, underwear and, of course, yellow raincoats being sold. Also sacks of peanuts with the same logo. And I am told that a new computer game is going to feature the running, raincoated phantom."

Saphira motioned to a delegate--a large, buxom woman, plain and without nuts but with peanuts, wearing one of the T-shirts. The woman joined Saphira in the foreground. "This is Matilda, and she's the president of the fan club. How did this thing happen? You don't know the young man in the raincoat. You don't know what he's like, where he's been, what he's read, what he's touched, or who he's slept with, so why all the sudden interest?"

Matilda pushed the glasses up on her nose. "He's dreamy, isn't he?" She giggled, and the crowd around them exploded with screams.

Saphira talked to the camera above the hubbub. "We have a clip ready to roll of reactions from other delegates to the young man in the raincoat. Can we run that now, Chester?"

The video clip provided rapid, consecutive person-on-the-street opinions.

A female delegate from California: "Isn't he dreamy?"

A male delegate from California: "Isn't he dreamy?"

An elderly woman from Arizona: "He reminds me of my grandson. Especially when my grandson goes out in the rain."

A Massachusetts woman carrying a poodle: "He needs to be free and wild, just like the sea. If they don't chase him, maybe he wouldn't run."

A female delegate from Oregon: "Nice raincoat."

A male delegate from Oregon: "I'd like to know where he stands on balancing the federal budget."

A female delegate from the District of Columbia: "I'd caucus with him any day of the week."

A woman dressed as a cheerleader from Texas: "He's so athletic. He's a real hero."

A man with a bandaged head, an arm in a sling, and a leg in a cast, balancing himself with crutches: "He's a menace to society. It was his fault that a tuba player in the convention band fell on me."

A female delegate from Tennessee: "He's so dreamy. Just like Elvis."

Mandy of Generation X-Crement: "Tablets."

A nun: "He's probably a very nice person when you get to know him."

A Nevada woman in a jogging suit: "Once in a while, a man comes along who makes you feel that it's okay to try one more blind date. He's that kind of guy. Ya, he's dreamy, all right."

A female delegate from Maryland: "He's got sex appeal. And that's something that even Congress can't repeal."

The camera switched live to Saphira Pitchfork and the group behind her shrieked happily. Saphira nodded. "I guess we're seeing a legend in the making."

Chester's mood was serious when the telecast returned to him. Calmly but emphatically, he reported, "Rumors continue to fly about what the young man in the raincoat is carrying. The reports have ranged from a revolver and a sword to an assault rifle and a heat-seeking stinger missile.

Here's what we do know. The convention security police
have asked delegates to cooperate in the investigation and
in the search for the young man in the raincoat. The
security police also ask that delegates refrain from
purchasing souvenir yellow raincoats, the wearing of which
could lead to unnecessary confusion, many false arrests and
unauthorized frisks."

CHAPTER 8
The Interview

With his usual debonair flair, candidate Andrew Chalk
greeted reporters Bella Wing and Mike Troy, and an UGH
News camera crew, at the door of his hotel suite.

"I'm so sorry I haven't been over to the convention hall
yet, but I'm glad you could come for this exclusive
interview," Chalk said, ushering them into the living room
area where the camera crew began to set up the equipment.

Chalk was neatly dressed in a dark blue suit with a red,
white and blue tie. The hotel room was luxuriously
furnished, and also very neat.

Bella noted the neatness with a tone of surprise, "I
imagined your personal headquarters to be cluttered with
speech drafts, strategy plans, and empty pizza delivery
boxes."

Chalk winked at her. "I knew TV was coming, so I
shoved all of that stuff in the bedroom, dining room, and
kitchen area," he confessed. The doors to all of those rooms
were closed. "It's been a busy place around here. Delegates
coming and going. Campaign staff coming and going.
Maids coming and going."

"So, you've been steadily campaigning?" Mike asked.

"That's right. The campaign isn't over until the last votes are counted. And there are still some votes out there for me to get, you know," Chalk said, smiling.

The camera crew indicated their readiness, so Bella directed Chalk to a plush sofa chair. Mike sat on one side on the end of a couch and Bella sat on Chalk's other side on another sofa. Mike started to lean back on the couch, but then stopped suddenly, felt along the back pillow and pulled out a woman's high-heel shoe.

Chalk laughed. "Oh, that's my wife's. She leaves those everywhere." Chalk, like lots of candidates, followed a traditional rule in case something unexplainable, embarrassing or downright illegal surfaced from his personal life: Put the blame on the wife.

At the cued time, the camera began to film the interview session, and Bella introduced the candidate, told about the nature of the interview, and used the word "exclusive" about 10 times.

Bella: "Mr. Chalk, you have not yet visited the convention hall. Is that a campaign ploy to build excitement about your eventual arrival? And don't you worry that Dr. Nebulan, whose been courting delegates at the convention, may outmaneuver you in delegate votes?"

Chalk: "We have different approaches. Dr. Nebulan likes crowds. I prefer a one-on-one setting. I have had many uncommitted delegates up here and I can assure you that they have all left with a different feeling about me."

Mike: "And your wife is at the convention..."

Chalk: "My lovely wife is at the convention, meeting with people, talking issues, exchanging recipes."

Mike: "Critics, namely the voters, have said that this election seems more about personalities than issues, and many people don't know where you or any of the candidates stand."

Chalk: "Well, I stand right here, though I'm sitting right now as your viewers can plainly see." (He looked directly at the camera.) "Hello, America. I love you all."

Bella: "We'd like to mention some issues and obtain a definite 'yes' or 'no' if we could."

Chalk (nodding): "I believe in answering issues forthright and frankly."

Bella: "Okay. How about the three-day weekend?"

Chalk: "Well, now that depends on which three days. Basically, I favor it."

Bella: "The gambling channel on TV."

Chalk: "I'd have to look into that one. With or without condom advertising? It could make a difference."

Bella: "Virtual reality government."

Chalk: "For it. If people can believe in government when there really isn't government, what harm could it do. It works for Santa Claus, doesn't it?"

Bella: "The proposed dirt pipeline from Colorado to Rhode Island."

Chalk: "If Colorado wants a lower elevation and Rhode Island wants a bigger state, and the rest of the taxpayers don't have to pay for it, I see no reason why dirt shouldn't flow back East. There should be enough dirt for everyone, enough dirt to go around."

Bella: "National Centrist Day."

Chalk: "People don't want gridlock. They want consensus. They want the middle ground, even if the middle ground lands to right of Genghis Khan. Look, people want decisions in the center. That way no one is really happy with the results, and so it is fair to everyone. Yes, I'm for the holiday and observance."

Bella: "The prison on the moon."

Chalk: "I favor it. If we can get criminals off the planet, I'm definitely for it. But the management of the prison should be done by a private company. And the project could give new life to the space program."

Bella: "Metric system implementation in Wisconsin."

Chalk: "I'm really not prepared to answer. I need to talk to the Wisconsin delegates at the convention first. I love the Wisconsin cheese and dairy products."

Bella: "The federal deficit."

Chalk: "As the federal deficit is now, our children's children's children's children will have to pay for it. And I say, 'Good.' Then they won't be spending their money on parties and bad music."

Bella: "A balanced budget."

Chalk: "Well, I'm for it because balancing it helps Wall Street and that helps me. But I must say, I'm rather baffled as to why so many average Americans out in middle America are for it. I mean, do they think once it is balanced, they are going to get anything from it. A tax cut or something? Heck, in balancing the budget, a lot of expense for the federal government will just be shifted to the state governments or individual themselves. But it's dog-gone cute to see so many average Americans hoodwinked by politicians and big business into thinking that it will be good for them. If politicians really wanted to do something fast about balancing the budget, they could just call a moratorium to the mounting interest debt, tell the banking industry they should be a little patriotic and help out their government, and wipe the slate clean. Of course, my friends in the banking industry would have a cow about that, so I couldn't support it, either. Just forget I ever mentioned it.

Bella: "Mongolia statehood."

Chalk: "I'd have to see how that affects the look of the stars on our flag. I'd rather mess with the Constitution than the flag--it's a national symbol."

Bella: "Performance art in the national parks."

Chalk: "I say that we don't need to see leaves numbered, geyser water colored with fake dead-animal blood, and grizzlies wearing bandannas. It's not natural. I know art when I see it and unnatural nature isn't art."

Mike: "Kleptomaniacs' rights."

Chalk: "I favor a 'don't ask/don't offer an excuse' policy. It's a tough issue. I know kleptomaniacs. Some are good people; some have even voted for me. But I have a problem with their rights extending to our armed services. We have to be able to keep our military weapons safe and accounted for. The issue needs to be studied."

Mike: "The disinformation superhighway."

Chalk: "There is something really exciting about being able to access wrong information from any person in any place around the world."

Mike: "Emu and ostrich subsidies."

Chalk: "We've got to be able to compete in a world emu and ostrich market. I'm for it."

Mike: "Gun sales to foreign juvenile delinquents."

Chalk: "It's not guns that kill people. It's foreign juvenile delinquents. We need to maintain a free trade with all countries. It makes us a stronger nation economically. It gives our big business the huge profits that they need, so they can at least feel good about something. It's the humane thing to do for our businesspeople. It's really a human rights issue. Big businesspeople are human, too. At least, partly."

Mike: "The death penalty."

Chalk: "The good book speaks to that issue--an eye for an

eye. The most modern version, translated by that bunch of counter-culture poets and music video pundits and on the bestseller list for 20 weeks, calls it 'a butt for a butt.' Regardless of the language, I agree. Besides, how can anyone be against the death penalty when they hear about that evil mass murderer in New York City who savagely massacred 50 innocent bystanders."

Mike: "UGH NEWS reporter Saphira Pitchfork looked into that story about the mass murderer and she found it to be totally false. So, why do you continue to use that story as support for the death penalty?"

Chalk, pondering a moment: "Well, maybe it wasn't New York City. It could have been Los Angeles. Yes, I think it was.

Mike: "Where do you stand on the gooseberry boycott?"

Chalk: "I couldn't live without my gooseberry jam in the morning. And Pintyler's Gooseberry Jam was very gracious in supporting my campaign with a generous donation."

The reporters paused, and Chalk, thinking he'd handled the interview with skill, leaned back comfortably in the chair and sighed with relief. Then he noticed reporter Mike Troy give a subtle nod to reporter Bella Wing, a signal that reminded Chalk of the scene from the old movie "Willard" where the guy yells to all his pet rats to tear up the mean boss. That was a "tear him up" signal which Chalk had seen once before. He'd seen it in an UGH news segment about a year ago, when the same news team descended, like rats after cheese, upon a little, old lady who ran a home for runaway children. The ambush interview caused the little, old lady to cry and admit that she'd failed to pay an overdue library book fine 50 years earlier. Gossipy celebrity magazines called Wing and Troy the "most watch-able couple on TV." Now Chalk remembered, and he began to shudder as Bella resumed the questioning.

Bella: "Mr. Chalk, how would you describe your moral fiber?"

Chalk: "Well...well...I believe in fiber. It is good for a person's diet, I know that."

Mike: "Have you ever watched a pornographic movie?"

Chalk: "I...I...I..Well, you know some matters involve youthful transgressions. Things we did when we were young and immature."

Mike: "You mean back in high school and college days, when you were in your teens and twenties."

Chalk: "Yes, and thirties and forties."

Mike: "Have you ever told a filthy joke in mixed company?"

Chalk: "I...I don't see what that has to do with the issues of this campaign."

Mike: "It's just a question. If you'd prefer not to answer, I'm sure the people watching this at home will understand."

Mike: "Have you ever worn a jock strap backwards?"

Chalk: "No comment."

Bella: "Have you ever beaten your wife?"

Chalk: "Certainly not. Unless you mean in chess or something."

Bella: "So you admit to it."

Chalk: "In chess or something. Occasionally, darts."

Bella: "Do you know a woman named Bonny Delton Pin?"

Chalk: "I do not!"

Bella: "She was your fourth-grade teacher."

Chalk: "Oh, oh. I guess she was."

Bella: "Do you know a Tisha St. Clough?"

Chalk: "I do not!"

Bella: "She's the niece of your fourth-grade teacher and

she says she has a college friend named Gloria Upland. Do you know her?"

Chalk: "I've never heard of her."

Bella: "She's a contributor to your campaign. You haven't heard of your own contributors? Do you know what she contributed?"

Chalk: "I...I...no, I don't. Some money, I imagine."

Mike: "Have you ever been involved in a hit and run?"

Chalk: "Certainly not."

Mike: "Have you ever bought drugs from a street corner hooker named Zoosie who wears tight leather jeans and a ruby red tank top?"

Chalk: "Absolutely not."

Mike: "Have you ever teased a dog?"

Chalk: "Well, well. Maybe, but just once or twice."

Mike: "Bought drugs from a hooker named Zoosie or teased a dog?"

Chalk: "Teased a dog! Maybe a poodle or a Pekingese."

Bella: "Did you know that the woman who contributed to your campaign owns a poodle and the hooker on the street corner owns a Pekingese?"

Chalk: "So what? Lots of people do."

Bella: "How did you know that they owned those dogs?"

Chalk: "I...I didn't. Just a guess, I guess."

Bella: "You guess?"

Chalk: "I guess. Yes. A guess. Yes."

Bella: "Have you ever been with a woman other than your wife."

Chalk: "Yes...I mean, no...I mean, I'm with you right now and you're a woman, according to sex anyway, and you're a woman other than my wife."

Bella: "You mentioned 'sex.' Are you familiar with the term 'sex kitten'? Do you talk about sex a lot?"

Chalk: "I...I...I...I...I...I...I..."

Mike: "If you don't care to answer, I'm sure the people watching this at home will understand."

Chalk suddenly became ballistic. He yelled at the reporters, "What's the meaning of this line of questioning?! I resent this attempt at character assassination based upon innuendo, cheap shots, and apparently peeking through my curtains. Especially coming from two reporters such as you." Chalk pulled a note pad from the hidden pocket inside his suit coat, and he shook his finger at Mike. "After all, wasn't it you, Mr. Troy, who failed to call your mother on Thanksgiving Day six years ago? The mother who gave you life, nursed you through the measles, and paid for your dental work?"

Mike suddenly broke into tears, covering his face with his hands.

Chalk turned to Bella, whose face expressed anticipated anguish. "And wasn't it you, Ms. Wing, who failed to report on your tax returns the $25 you won in scratch-ticket lotto game two years ago. Isn't that the truth? And nothing but the truth?"

Bella was reduced to tears. She cried uncontrollably into a hankie.

Chalk spoke to the camera. "I think TV history was made today, don't you? The interviewee makes the interviewers cry."

The interview session ended, with Bella and Mike embracing as they continued to blubber. The camera crew gathered up the gear, and Chalk held the door open as everyone from the UGH news team exited humbly. Chalk watched them walk down the hallway. The sound of sobs from Bella and Mike faded away.

Candidate Chalk then grinned, closed the door, and

rubbed his hands together with anxious joy.

He announced loudly, "They're gone, everybody! You can come out now!"

Coming out into the hotel's living room from all doors, from the bedroom, bathroom, kitchen, and even two closets were women in bathing suits or tight sweaters and mini-skirts. They filled the living room. Some wore campaign hats. Some were convention band members and carried instruments. Some held bottles of champagne and blew on party noise-makers. Some threw confetti. Their previous silence in hiding was replaced by loud, festive partying.

Chalk cheerfully took a woman in each of his arms and squeezed them playfully as they laughed. Chalk knew what he liked most about politics--the support of the party.

CHAPTER 9
The Speech

Josh Deaver, the Ameriminds candidate who planned to withdraw from the nomination race prior to the delegate vote count, stood at the speaker's platform in the convention hall, waiting for a polite round of applause from the delegates to pass.

He waved pleasantly, but his face showed the typical disappointed exhaustion of a candidate who had worked hard but knew that victory was meant for someone else.

Chester Mega's voice could be heard, as the camera continued to show the waving candidate. "A class act for sure, but the Josh Deaver campaign just wasn't able to get into gear, attract the attention of the media or the voters, nor raise the funds from corporate giants. Let's listen now as he gives his final address."

Deaver began to speak, as the remaining applause ended, "Fellow Americans, friends of freedom and democracy and the best nation in the world, I ask you to..."

The UGH network interrupted the speech, televising a graphic for "a special news bulletin."

Chester was back on camera, with a flushed face and excited tone. "We need to break in here for a special news bulletin that is coming from the main office of this convention hall."

A little man wearing workman's clothing with the name "Bob" in stitched letters on his shirt waited for about 10 seconds of uncomfortable dead-air time before being prompted from the side that he could proceed with the announcement.

He read a short message, "Delegates are asked not to remove any of the potted plants from the convention lobby or hall. They are there for decorative purposes in order to make your visit here more pleasant. Also, taking them home or back to a hotel room would be a mistake because they have been sprayed with stinky fox urine."

Chester was back on camera, looking somewhat puzzled, but he sipped some coffee from a mug and directed the production people to return the telecast to Deaver's speech.

"...And I thank you all so much from the bottom of my heart," Deaver said in summation. The crowd cheered and bobbed campaign signs.

The telecast returned to Chester in the anchor booth. "Let me give a quick recap of what we've learned here today for those of you at home," Chester said. "The convention management has asked delegates to refrain from taking potted plants. The plants won't serve as good souvenirs of this convention because they've been sprayed with stinky fox urine." Chester took a deep breath and continued, "Candidate Josh Deaver announced his official withdrawal from the race for the Ameriminds presidential nomination. He said he has been unable to get his message out to the voters. He thanked the delegates for their support and freed them from having to vote for him on a first ballot. He said he cut his speaking time short in order to allow two fellow Ameriminds to speak about special, personal concerns. One is a homeless man named Tom, who is standing at the speaker's platform now, and the other will be a Montana cowboy named Boyd Larkspur. Let's go back down to hear what Tom the homeless man has to say."

A lean, hungry-looking man, in faded jeans and a tattered plaid shirt, stood tall and dignified as he looked with determination down from the podium to the quiet, huddled mass of curious delegates. The homeless man's hair was combed, in an attempt to be neat, but it was also obvious that his hair was shaggy and hadn't been cut for months. His face showed several days-worth of stubble. He wore a pair of black-rimmed glasses and the left-ear part of the frames was missing. His eyes were dull and tired. He looked older than his years. He had grown used to constant hunger and his teeth hurt because he couldn't afford to go to the dentist for needed dental work.

At first, Tom's voice was weak and lacked resonance. The truth was that he didn't talk much and, when he did, usually he was ignored. However, as he spoke honestly and "from the heart" to the delegates, a richness and power developed in his voice and he delivered the words with eloquence.

"I don't think too much about the American dream at this time in my life," he began. "I'm just trying to survive right now. I'm trying to stay physically and mentally healthy until that moment when someone, maybe one of you out there, is willing to throw me a life-line and give me an opportunity for employment. When I pass by houses--no, they are actually homes--all along a street, I think about the people who live inside, and dream that I will get a job and have a home one day, too."

Tom the homeless man continued, pulling some crumpled notes from his shirt pocket. "But I didn't come here to talk about myself. I came to tell you about some of the people I know. Some of the people don't have homes. Others do have homes and they still have additional needs. I know a couple named Kyle and Sue who support five children on minimum-wage salaries without public assistance. When Kyle lost his full-time job, he found temporary work. Then the family car broke down, followed by the washing machine and then the water heater in their home. Now Kyle and Sue skip their noon lunches, so they can save money for the unexpected expenses. They are good people. They deserve better."

Tom continued, "I know a woman named Dinah who works full-time, and dreams of going to college and studying to be a nurse. She can barely afford the cost of daycare for her daughter. There's no room in her budget for any extra item, such as a new toy for her daughter. She's a good person. She deserves better."

Tom described another acquaintance. "I know an 85-year-old woman named Mrs. Jones who lives alone, residing in a boarding house. After she pays her living expenses and buys monthly medications, she has no extra money. For her, going to a beauty salon and having her hair permed is a luxury. She's a good person. She deserves better."

The crowd remained attentive during Tom's speech. "I

know a man named Sidney who lives in a group home for the mentally ill. While the state provides a stipend, frequently it is not enough to meet his needs. Sidney appreciates gifts of toothpaste, shampoo, and disposable razors. He's a good person. He deserves better." The crowd applauded.

"I know a woman named Sarah who is in the middle of a divorce from an abusive husband. She's trying to care for her two children with a part-time job. She doesn't have a car and hopes to be able to buy a bicycle, so she can get to work with a little more ease. She's a good person. She deserves better." The crowd respectfully applauded again.

"I know a man named Clyde who works full-time and takes care of his ill wife and their three children. His only pair of shoes is held together with duct tape. He's a good person. He deserves better." At this point, Tom's eyes welled up and his voice cracked. The same mood moved through the crowd.

Tom continued, "I know a couple named Pete and May. Pete has been hospitalized several times from illness. May is awaiting a second surgery. Employed all their lives, they have no health insurance. Hospital bills remain unpaid, forcing May to postpone the next operation. They are good people. They deserve better."

Tom paused to keep his composure. "I knew a man named Ed. He was a friend. He died on a cold night on a cold street just last week. He left a note, saying that he wanted me to have his coat, so I could stay warmer this winter. He was a good person. He deserved better."

The crowd was silent and attentive. Some delegates wiped tears from their eyes.

Tom concluded, "These are just some of the people I know. I imagine you know people like them. These are the people of America, too. They are good people. We are here at this convention because we believe that the quality of life for people can and should be better. There are lots of people with needs and lots of people counting on us. Please don't forget any of them."

Tom the homeless man stepped back from the lectern and the convention crowd burst into applause and cheers. Flags and campaign signs were waved triumphantly.

Chester was wiping his eyes with a handkerchief as the telecast returned to him. "Certainly, an inspirational speech," he commented, sniffling. "About the first, good speech I've heard so far at this convention."

The camera view widened to show election analysts Herman Merdell and Frank Fink sitting next to Chester, who introduced them again to the viewing public and asked for their opinions of the speech.

Merdell was indignant. "I just found the whole thing irrelevant. Hearing about average Americans with problems is not my idea of a convention speech. It demeans most of the people who are here--people who have the money to travel to Kansas, relax in hotels for several days, and then have a little fun with politics. It demeans the people who are tired of hearing about problems and instead want to know what's good, profitable, and fat-free about America."

Fink was also critical. "It was too long."

Merdell continued, "I don't know why candidate Josh Deaver gave his time to someone like that. The main issue here is not whether Americans are having problems, but rather which candidate will gain from the Deaver withdrawal. The speech was a convention footnote, nothing more. Maybe even a shoeless footnote."

Fink responded, "It was too long."

Merdell elucidated with about as much skill as a sumo wrestler pole-vaulting, "I just don't think it will sell. It's a message without a messenger. A cart before the horse. Blood from a turnip. A bird in the bush. A day in the life of a great big yawn. A journey to the center of the earth. A sleep tight and don't let the bed bugs bite."

Fink added, "A partridge in a pear tree."

Chester summarized, "Thank you, gentlemen. I've never heard sour grapes brought to life so vividly before." The election analysts smiled appreciatively. "Despite the pooh-poohing about the speech, it continues to receive loud applause from the delegates. The longest applause I've heard so far at this convention," Chester added. "Let's check in with Trixie Spaniel on the convention floor."

When reporter Trixie Spaniel sought a statement from candidate Dr. Ross Nebulan, she raised her voice in order to be heard above the clamor of the enthusiastic crowd. "Dr. Nebulan, what's your opinion of the speech by Tom the homeless man?"

Nebulan responded loudly, "I knew an average person once and he was nothing like any of those people mentioned in the speech."

"Over to you, Hank," Trixie said.

Reporter Hank Midland was with candidate Joyce Hyphen Martindale. Hank asked, "How would you assess the speech, Ms. Hyphen Martindale?"

"Well, he is a man, seeing the world through a man's perspective. He referred to five men by name and only five women by name. Why not six women and four men, or seven women and three men? After all, there are more women in the world than men, more women suffering economic hardships than men, more women with children than men, more women in the labor force and more women forced into childbirth labor because of men."

Hyphen Martindale seized the microphone from Hank and elbowed him out of the picture, as she stared down the camera with an angry look. "And another thing. Tell those little male morons doing the election analyses that I make cookies when I damn well please." She displayed a tray of cookies.

Hank wrestled with her for the microphone, noting, "Oh...Oh my, cookies shaped like...like...they look like..."

Hyphen Martindale bluntly started to describe them, when Hank quickly pulled the microphone away and explained in safe language, "The private parts of men and women."

"That's right," bellowed Hyphen Martindale, tugging the microphone out of Hank's hand. "See if those two male moronic election analysts can analyze this," she growled, taking a male cookie in her hand and taking a bit out of it.

Hank cautioned her. "Violence, profanity and shower scenes from the rear are okay, especially if it is on a cop show, but, as a news organization, we can't show obscene cookies on the air. We'd have to use a blue dot to cover them."

Hyphen Martindale swung the microphone several times at the dodging reporter. Then she faced the camera again, smiled, and politely explained, "They are sugar cookies in different shapes. And some have almonds on the top." Abruptly, she glared savagely at Hank. "Which would you like? Male or female cookies?"

Hank gulped nervously. He didn't answer. "Over to you, Saphira."

Reporter Saphira Pitchfork was standing beside Cassie Chalk, wife of candidate Andrew Chalk. "Save a cookie for me," Saphira acknowledged. "Ms. Chalk..."

The candidate's wife interrupted. "Our French chef makes cookies all the time." She quickly added, as though worried about a misinterpretation, "But they are star and bell shapes."

Saphira frowned. "Yes...Well, how do you think your husband would react to the speech by Tom the homeless man?"

Mrs. Chalk paused, seriously considering the question and how her answer might affect her husband's chances, his entire career in public service, and her shopping sprees. "I think he would probably feel sorry for the poor man for not having a good speech writer."

Back at the hotel suite, Andrew Chalk, naked and in bed with a black-haired woman wearing a straw campaign hat with the words "New Mexico" along the front band, was preoccupied, talking over his phone. "Listen, Barney," Chalk ordered, "Find out if that homeless guy would like to work for me as a speech writer. Start with an offer of one square meal a day and, if he doesn't bite on that, you have my permission to raise the offer to two meals a day and a free VCR."

CHAPTER 10
The Proposal

Charla Willow was excited about the next episodes of her TV tabloid news show, "Sensations." She knew they would be big hits.

One program, with computer enhancements by Joey the cameraman, featured a simulation of what it would have been like if death-row prisoner James Cash Cathcart had been executed by lethal injection rather than in the electric chair. A gas chamber simulation was also in the works.

Another program featured the grand opening of an orphanage, privately owned and operated by a group of Republicans. Single, unwed mothers ready to give up their children would be given coupons for discounts on fast food meals and cable TV. Single, unwed fathers would be tortured in the basement. Rich people who didn't have time for their children and didn't want to spend the money to hire nannies would be offered tax credits for their children. The Republicans were pretty sure their orphanage business would result in franchises. They had faith in the power of supply and demand.

A third upcoming program provided shocking accusations that members of the Ameriminds judiciary caucus engaged in an orgy while they were in a secret, closed session, just a door away from the public meeting. The closed session lasted for more than an hour, and people waiting for them to return and reconvene the public meeting had a good question when they asked, "What else could they be doing in there?" A re-enactment of what could have happened was performed by a group of actors. In accordance with standards for the regular late-night time slot on most of the TV networks, ribbons and dots, appropriately placed by the show's graphics department, would be tastefully used to cover the physical locations and moments of X-rated activity. The ribbons and dots would be removed for the X-rated pay-for-view channels and the public access channels.

When Charla greeted Joey the cameraman at their hospitality room in the convention hall, Joey held up a videotape and said, "You'll want to see this. I recorded it for you."

"What's up?" Charla asked.

"Remember when we found that cowboy named Boyd something-or-other unconscious in the stairwell area?"

"Yes. And you took some film of him passed out on the floor, so we could later use it for a story about a love-lost Wyoming cowboy who died of a broken heart and too much booze at the convention. And you were going to computer-enhance the scene to make it look like a ghostly spirit, resembling Abraham Lincoln, was rising out of his body."

"Yes. That guy. But I think the cowboy was from Montana," Joey replied. "Anyway, we may have to hold that one and revise it for the Democratic or Republican conventions later this year."

"Why? What happened?" Charla took the videotape and slipped it into their combination television/VCR unit.

Joey provided an introductory explanation as the tape began to play. "Candidate Josh Deaver withdrew from the race and he allowed two other people to address the convention. One was a homeless guy and the other was that cowboy."

Charla started to watch the tape as it showed Boyd Larkspur, in his hat and western clothes, shaking hands with Tom the homeless man and then proceeding to the speaker's stand.

"Hello, I'm Boyd Larkspur and I'm from Montana," said the cowboy, nervous but mustering a smile as the Montana delegation cheered. "I'd like to tell you about a true love story."

Concentrating on the videotape, Charla folded her arms and relaxed her stance.

Boyd continued his speech. "I'm no speaker or anything. I'm just a common guy from the West. But it's important for me to do this, because I don't know what else to do. It seems like saying it public for the world to hear would mean something special and maybe help right some wrongs that I've done. Some of you may have recently seen me on TV. On TV with another woman I don't even know and a hairy chest that wasn't even mine. Well, that TV appearance was a mistake I made that has nearly cost me the most precious thing on earth. My beautiful Rosie."

The Connecticut delegation applauded.

Boyd continued, "About a year ago, Rosie and I met at a Missouri conference of campaign workers for Josh Deaver. And we rode the Deaver campaign bus together on the campaign trail all over Iowa. In Pottawattamie County, Rosie and I fell in love. Then I returned to Montana and Rosie returned to her home state of Connecticut. We kept in contact through letters and e-mail and even got back together for a fly-fishing trip in Montana and a Star Trek convention in Connecticut. Because Rosie and I both became delegates to this convention, our plan was to, yes, get married right here."

A sprinkling of applause interrupted his speech.

Charla's mouth dropped open and she looked with complete surprise at Joey. Joey just nodded.

Boyd continued, "Well, I kind of goofed up and complicated the matter. My good intentions got scrambled in the egg beater of TV life. But Rosie McCoy, I love you more than the sun can shine and the wind can blow."

The TV camera focused upon a pretty, young woman in the Connecticut delegation, who was wiping tears of joy from her eyes. With printed words at the bottom of the picture, the telecast designated her as "Rosie McCoy, Connecticut delegate."

"Rosie," Boyd asked, "Would you marry me?"

The convention delegates cheered and whistled with approval.

The camera returned to Rosie, who was nodding her head affirmatively and mouthing the word "Yes."

The band began to play a lively version of "Happy Days Are Here Again."

At that point, Boyd threw his hat in the air, hurried down the back way of the speaker's platform and sprinted into the crowd. The telecast split into two separate camera views, one showing Boyd, one showing Rosie. Boyd and Rosie eagerly rushed toward each other. Through the sections of delegates, they jogged.

The telecast then split into 12 separate camera views, one showing Boyd, one showing Rosie, and the other 10 showing reporters and camera people, all hurrying through the crowd, toward the point where Rosie and Boyd would meet.

In the Arkansas section, Rosie jumped into Boyd's outstretched arms and he swung her around, her legs hitting an Arkansas delegate and knocking him to the side. Then Rosie and Boyd embraced with a hug and a long kiss.

Charla looked at Joey. "You mean it was true? A true love story?"

Joey nodded.

The videotape showed that reporter Trixie Spaniel was first on the scene, declaring "dibs" on the couple, who was still locked in a kiss, as other reporters arrived.

Finally, Trixie physically separated the beaming, lovesick couple and then lodged herself and the microphone between them, as her cameraman focused in close.

Charla shouted at the videotape, "That reporter got my story!"

"How do you feel right now?" Trixie asked the couple.

Boyd gave a wide "Aw-Shucks!" kind of grin and Rosie glowed with the usual radiance of a bride-to-be. "Happy," Rosie replied.

Trixie stepped back from the couple, as reporters converged upon them from all sides, resembling a pack of wolves circling and gnawing away at a downed deer.

Trixie faced the camera, glancing occasionally at papers on her clipboard. "This is a love story," reported Trixie. "A love story about a Democrat from Montana and a Republican from Connecticut who are in love during a great and glorious political drama."

"That was my story! That was my idea!" yelled Charla at the videotape.

Trixie continued, "From what we can gather at this time, this is quite a unique story because Boyd and Rosie have such different backgrounds. Boyd is from Montana, a Democrat-turned Amerimind; Rosie is from Connecticut, a Republican-turned Amerimind. Boyd is interested in the issues of social programs, domestic policy, and wind and solar energy; Rosie is interested in the issues of defense spending, foreign policy, and nuclear power. Boyd eats beef; Rosie is a vegetarian. Boyd has a dog; Rosie has a cat. Boyd drives a Chevy; Rosie drives a Ford. Boyd likes rodeos; Rosie likes operas. Boyd won't ask for directions; Rosie will."

Pausing as the camera showed Boyd and Rosie battling their way through the mob of reporters, Trixie concluded, "Isn't love wonderful?"

Charla pushed the VCR button, stopping the tape. "I've

seen enough. Real-life really makes me mad. It is so unpredictable!"

CHAPTER 11
The Raincoat Fad

Harry Hooper fumed. He couldn't believe his eyes. The convention security headquarters was filled with young men in yellow raincoats, each being questioned by security officers.

And not just young men in raincoats. There were old men in raincoats, young women in raincoats, old women in raincoats, and people of every color, size, religion, disability, sexual orientation, economic status, and fashion statement in raincoats.

Harry seethed. He never thought his investigative skills would be hindered by a fad. A raincoat fad!

The idea of the mysterious and probably dangerous original young man in a raincoat gaining national folk hero status made Harry angry and more determined than ever to catch the fugitive.

Harry had faced a lot of challenges before and had always prevailed. Like the time when he intercepted a teenage groupie as she was trying to sneak into the dressing room of the rock group "Ugly Sad Onions" during one concert season. Or the time Harry stopped a fanatic mule rights activist from trying to pin a tail on one of the Jaycee participants in the donkey basketball game. Then there was the time at the huge silent book auction when Harry had to break up a fight between two truculent book-buyers who wanted the same "self-help" book.

And Harry especially remembered the time a faith healer

freaked out while performing a Gregorian chant at a revival meeting and started clobbering a sick woman with a collection plate. Harry subdued the rabid faith healer and credited the use of a hymnal as making the difference. He told the press, "When it comes to impact, a collection plate is no match for a hymnal." Fortunately, the woman healed with 10 stitches on the noggin and a $100,000 legal settlement. The faith healer went to an entrepreneurial treatment center, attends Faith Healers Anonymous regularly, and now leads a productive life as an insurance salesman. But, to this day, he gets sympathy pains when someone sings "Bringing in the Sheaves."

Harry knew he lived a rough and tumble life. It came with the territory. Security is a tough job, but somebody has to do it. He had the battle scars.

One time, while providing security at the filming of an infommercial for a buffalo beef jerky processor, he got caught in the line of fire when 20 women from the audience stampeded over him to get to the order table. Another time, he had to throw his body into a drunken, bellicose salesman wielding a socket wrench during a tool convention. Harry still had a socket scar on his lower abdomen.

However, Harry could call himself a "survivor." Just like the latest episode when he fell to the convention floor after the giant TV screen toppled. He escaped injury. In fact, so did the young man in the raincoat. But their good fortune was partly thanks to their landing on a slow-moving group of disoriented Florida delegates.

Harry was still mad that the Ameriminds national committee was considering sending a partial bill for the screen to the convention hall security office. It was the young man in the raincoat who led the way and plowed into the screen. Harry believed that if they'd sprayed the screen with stinky fox urine, maybe the young man in the raincoat would have avoided it altogether.

Harry watched as an old woman in a raincoat was led away by a security officer to the finger-print room. Though their targeted fugitive in the raincoat had not yet been found, the dragnet had been pretty successful. Sixty-five raincoats were confiscated, as well as fourteen cans of graffiti spray paint, six pea-shooters, and a dangerous tuba.

The security team also uncovered Jim Bob Grinch, an annoying Republican politician who admitted he was acting as a mole in the large California delegation, spying on the Ameriminds caucus and their frequent enjoyment of double-dip ice cream cones.

Harry told Grinch that there wasn't anything secretive enough about the caucus that deserved another Republican scandal. In fact, the caucus' agenda pretty much represented the way the Ameriminds Party differed from the other two parties. The Ameriminds double-dip ice cream cones actually contained two scoops of ice cream. The Democratic version provided two scoops at a little higher cost so that a third scoop would go to someone who couldn't afford it. The Republican version used the double-dip reference, while it provided only one scoop of ice cream.

Politics, however, didn't mean much to Harry. He had always led an apolitical life. He found it to be most compatible with security work. He believed in democracy, but he'd never practiced it on others. That's probably why Harry released the pompous Republican politician from the custody of the security office, but on "Harry Hooper's terms." For decades, Harry had always wanted to shave someone's head and put the person on a plane to Vietnam. So, that's what Grinch had to agree to, in return for a full pardon from the security office and a promise that the infiltration story wouldn't be leaked to the press until after the election.

With annoyance, Harry took special notice of a loud, disruptive drunk who was struggling between two security officers. The officers kept him from falling on his face. The intoxicated delegate, who described himself as a judge from Texas, railed about his guilt in a murder and the innocence of the recently executed death-row inmate James Cash Cathcart.

Harry, at the end of his emotional rope, had more than he could stand. "What's going on here?" Harry demanded. The officers explained that the drunk had wandered into the security office and wasn't even wearing a raincoat.

Harry shook his head with disgust. Then Harry grabbed the drunk by the cuff of the collar, told him to "Go sleep it off," and hurled him out the security office door. With orders to his security officers, Harry barked, "We have real work to do around here. If they aren't in a raincoat, don't waste your time with them."

CHAPTER 12
Nomination Night Jitters

UGH News anchorman Chester Mega was somewhat breathless as he excitedly but professionally reported the latest news.

He loved special news bulletins because they always made him feel like a kid who gets to tell something first, ahead of others. Chester realized that special news bulletins are a privilege for the messenger. Knowing something that others don't know is power. That's why, to this day, Chester felt good about taking the zoology course way back in college and learning about gnus. He knew what others didn't know about gnus. Chester was the expert on gnu news. He also knew new gnu news from old gnu news. And, since power translates into control, he intended to tell who he wanted when he wanted.

Chester always thought of power as the TV remote control of life. Click it on and the range of channels is at least 40. Hundreds if there's a satellite dish. Click it off and life takes on a different meaning. It means not knowing what life is like beyond the next channel, on the other side of the hill. It means not knowing who did what, when and where, why and how or with how much, unless you have a subscription to the newspaper or can find your way online in a computer network. It means not knowing what the final "Jeopardy" answer will be. Answers are what people strive to attain. They are treasure. Chester was a firm believer and knew that TV provided all the answers if you just had the right questions.

Chester proudly understood the scope of TV. After all, television is more than just a noisy box in the living room. It is a culture. The TV culture provides participants with the opportunity for the shared experience of watching a dim-witted, half-hour situation comedy with millions of other people. Entertainment, news, sports, spirituality, shopping, and more; TV can furnish it all at the touch of a button and the payment of a cable bill, Chester marveled.

Chester knew people who referred to themselves as "African American," "Native American," "Asian American," "Irish American," "Gay American," "Rich American," and other designations relating to culture, ethnicity, preference, or status. For Chester, it was very simple. He preferred just "Television American."

Chester read the special news bulletin as it scrolled on his teleprompter. "A group of flip-floppies has forcibly taken over a hospitality bar near the lobby area in this convention hall. It is reported that they are highly inebriated--heck, they are as drunk as skunks--and they are trying to have their way with the liquor supply. A bartender who knows how to mix the drinks has been taken hostage. A security force is converging on the site and UGH News will bring you live footage of the chaos and violence just as soon as one of our reporters gets there. And I should remind our reporters who can hear me now, by way of our high-tech and expensive radio equipment, that the first one who gets there wins additional points toward the trip to Yellowstone Park and the last one who gets there is a rotten egg."

Saphira Pitchfork's picture appeared, as the live TV coverage of the event cut in. Saphira was in the middle of the bar, with security officers and flip-floppies engaged in hand-to-hand combat all around her, trashing the tables and chairs. Saphira's picture was shaky and she occasionally disappeared from view as the cameraman holding the camera was pushed or dodged the brawling activity. Saphira shouted, "I'm first, Chester." However, before she could begin her report, she pointed and shouted to her cameraman, "Watch out!" At that point, a crashing sound was immediately followed by shattered glass raining onto the camera, and the camera view suddenly took a nose-dive into the floor. The cameraman apparently was knocked out cold by an assailant brandishing a wine bottle.

"Apparently, we've lost our video," Chester understated. To compensate, he held up a portrait photo of reporter Saphira and the anchor booth camera closed in upon the photo as Saphira's voice was heard.

"It's a rocky time in the old bar tonight," Saphira reported loudly, "There are...there are people fighting all around us...A lot of furniture has...has been damaged beyond repair and…watch out! Get your hands off me, you big..." The audio went dead.

"Apparently, we've lost our audio," Chester said, putting down Saphira's photo. "Please stand by for that. In the meantime, for those of you watching who may not know much about the flip-floppies, let me try to explain the generation moods. In the 1960s, there were the hippies-- peace-loving, long-haired, freaky people with profane mouths--followed by the yippies of the 1960s and 1970s, who were just as hairy but more violence-prone and mean-spirited, in a Molotov cocktail kind of way. In the 1980s, there were the yuppies, the selfish and apathetic group of groomed people in business suits. The early 1990s had mopies--people who sat around moping about everything despite their good fortune and not having to face the prospect of being drafted. Now, the flip-floppies are the rage. They are mainly made up of people from all of the other groups who sold-out one way or another and who have flip-flopped in their principles or never had any to begin with. Flip-floppies shouldn't be confused with the nerdy group of computer enthusiasts known as disk floppies."

Holding a piece of paper, a hand of someone hiding below the anchor desk appeared just left of Chester in camera view. The hand rattled the paper to get Chester's attention. Chester took the piece of paper and the hand disappeared out of sight.

"This just in," Chester said, reading the note.

"Apparently, we've lost our reporter and cameraman who
has been taken into custody and transported downtown to
the county jail with others at the disturbance."

Holding a piece of paper with the toes, a foot appeared to
the left of Chester in camera view. Chester took the sheet of
paper and the foot disappeared out of sight. "A footnote,"
Chester qualified. "Although our reporter and cameraman
did nothing wrong, the UGH Network is not responsible for
their conduct or welfare in times of controversy."

Chester continued to read, "Go to a commercial." Chester
stopped, embarrassed, and laughed, "Oh, we need to take a
commercial break." He gave his fatherly, comforting smile.

FIRST COMMERCIAL: A car salesman slowly walked
through his large lot. "We've got another beaut, here, at
Ted's Global Automotive City. This time, a small compact
car from Japan." He tapped on the hood, but then stopped
because he was making a dent. "This car is so compact that
it can be disassembled and transported in any large
suitcase. This is a businessperson's dream car. Got to take a
plane trip? Well, just take your car with you on the trip.
Assemble it when you get there and you avoid the cost of
rental cars. Instructions for re-assembly come in plain
Japanese. Hurry on down. And ask about our 15-mile
guarantee."

SECOND COMMERCIAL: A sweet, young woman was
softly humming as she applied Make-Me-Happy Roll-On
Deodorant to her underarms. Then she danced around the
room, singing, "Make-Me-Happy sure makes me happy.
And it makes Gunther happy, too. And Jake. And Kilroy,
Lee, Glen, Boris, and Pierre." She blew a kiss, sensuously
saying, "And how about you?"

THIRD COMMERCIAL: A talk show host presented a

short preview of an upcoming program. "Have you ever wanted to punch a tall person right in the nose? Or maybe the knee cap? We'll talk with short people who have done it. Short people with even shorter fuses. Join me, Calamity Jane McLaine, on 'Talk Until We Drop' this Thursday on your local channel. Short people, tall people, and the potential for violence. Don't miss it."

Reporter Mike Troy began his report from the hospitality bar that was the site of convention disruption by flip-floppies. Most the room's furniture was smashed, mirrors were shattered, and the glass of broken bottles was everywhere. The room was still being cleared of drunken flip-floppies by the police. Mike was speaking with the bartender, who had been a hostage.

"What was it like in this awful hell hole?" Mike asked dramatically.

The bartender bristled a bit. "No different from the convention of school librarians several months ago. However, they did create quite a mess."

"What happened in this awful hell hole?"

"Well, I think it all started when one, small group of flip-floppies started pushing each other while arguing about who'd get the last pretzel. I don't know who they were. Three long-haired guys, two short-haired women, and one unidentified walking object. A guy pulled out a knife and threatened to kill the next person who reached for the pretzel. Geez! Used to be they'd kill you for a quarter. Nowadays, they'll kill you for a pretzel. Heck, they'll kill you for an I.O.U. It's just crazy."

"Is that when all hell broke loose?"

"Sure was. And everybody joined in, because this group is all a bunch of joiners, you know. One person does it and they all have to do it. I've seen lemmings with more individuality. And I'm not sure what happened to the pretzel."

Mike moved to a witness--a large, stout member of the convention band carrying a tuba.

"You saw what happened in this hell hole?"

"Yep. Just sitting at the bar with my tuba, minding my own business and soaking up the suds. You know, when there are flip-floppies around, what one does, they all imitate. It was real unfortunate for the guy who took the first punch and then received all the following imitation punches. The only thing that protected me from the ruckus was my tuba."

"How so?"

"Every time they came close, I let them have it with a loud, flat note," he said, gently stroking the tuba. "Does wonders with head-aching drunks, every time."

Mike moved to another witness--a mean-looking, tattoo-covered member of a motorcycle gang, who was wearing black leather and assorted spikes and medallions.

"What happened in this hell hole?"

The gang member launched into an angry description peppered with profanity that had to be deleted from the broadcast through the technological use of appropriately placed "beeps."

"That (beep) guy over there was (beep) thumped by that (beep) (beep) group of (beep) (beep) (beep). Then the whole (beep) joint took a (beep) in a fighting kind of way and (beep) (beep) (beep). Then that (beep) tuba kept (beep) (beep) and (beep) were falling like (beep) in a (beep) (beep). 'Course, I didn't think the (beep) (beep) thing was a (beep) tuba. I (beep) thought it was a (beep) guy who'd (beep) eaten too (beep) much (beep) chili around here.

Then (beep) (beep) (beep) (beep) (beep) (beep) (beep) (beep) (beep)."

Mike addressed the camera. "A lot of blue notes down here, at the site of a major riot during this convention. Back to you, Chester."

"Thanks, Mike," Chester responded. From above, a hand with a sheet of paper came into camera view over Chester's head and he promptly reached up and took the note. "This just in," he said, reading the note. "Following their strip-search, UGH News reporter Saphira Pitchfork and her cameraman were released from the county jail."

Suddenly, UGH News workers' hands with notes sprang from every direction at Chester. He sat there befuddled, surrounded from left to right, top to bottom, with hands urgently shaking pieces of paper at him.

"Let's go to Bella Wing, in a meeting room adjacent to the convention floor," Chester said, fending off the chaos in the anchor booth.

"Chester, I am standing here at what was the first official debate of the candidates' wives and significant others. Three more debates are planned during the campaign. This debate really provided no surprises, but the tone did get sassy and mean-spirited at several times and we made sure to include those clips for the viewing public. The debate involved Cassie Chalk, wife of candidate Andrew Chalk; Reva Nebulan, wife of candidate Ross Nebulan; and Mindy Bundiff Gadfly, the significant other representing candidate Joyce Hyphen Martindale."

The first clip of the debate was shown. Mindy Bundiff Gadfly questioned the feminist determination of the other two women, asking why neither used their original last name.

Reva: "I don't use mine because it was 'Snotwhiner' and I was anxious most of early life to get another name. Besides, I made the choice to take my husband's name. That was my choice. By using my father's last name, is that supposed to mean I am an 'independent woman?' I had more choice in the matter when I took my husband's name."

Mindy: "Why didn't you take your mother's name?"

Reva: "Because it was 'Stinkbadder.' Would you want a name like that?"

Cassie: "I don't use my own last name because it is 'White' and that would make me 'Cassie White Chalk' which I don't think sounds very inclusive."

Another clip showed an exchange about the claim to represent average women.

Cassie: "You say you're an average woman. Isn't that a big, fat lie?"

Reva: "My weight is none of your business. I like to do average things like average women. Like...like...sewing. Just the other day, I sewed a button on my Jacques Renoir Import."

Cassie: "I crochet. Do you crochet?"

Reva: "Occasionally. I do enjoy it. But it is rather difficult to hit the ball through each little, wire hoop."

Mindy: "Admit it. You both are rich and you don't even know the price of a jar of caviar."

A third clip showed responses from the women about the candidates.

Mindy: "Joyce Hyphen Martindale is a woman of strength and character. I've seen her pick a fight with an auto mechanic, just for the hell of it. I've seen her perform the Heimlich Maneuver on men who weren't even choking. She's tough. She'll get the job done. I've seen her go to bat for old bats like you and still you don't support her."

Reva: "She's a character, all right. The Nebulan family represents the values of America. And I'd like to take this moment to send heart-felt greetings to our two children, who are away at reform school; my encounter group; the wonderful people at the substance abuse center; and Ben the plumber. Maybe my husband doesn't know any homeless people, but he has the ability to solve real problems of real people."

Cassie: "Your husband couldn't pound nails through snow. My husband has worked hard for the nomination. I don't doubt that he's with a voter right this very minute."

Cassie Chalk missed the mark this time. Back at the hotel suite, her husband was naked and in bed with a blond woman whose admission caused him consternation.

"You mean you aren't a voting delegate at all?" he said. "You're just a non-voting maid here at the hotel?"

With a pouting expression, the woman nodded.

Andrew Chalk scratched his chin and made a political decision. "Well," he replied. "I guess I should look at it as my post-nomination effort. After all, when I get the nomination of the Ameriminds Party delegates tomorrow, I'll have to start campaigning on a nationwide basis." He looked at her and she smiled with approval. "I guess it wouldn't hurt to start that national campaign a bit earlier," he added, suddenly happy with his reasoning. She smiled again and anxiously opened her arms to him.

Reporter Bella Wing summed up the first debate of the candidates' women for the UGH News viewers. "It was stupid."

Then she introduced May Dell Deaver, wife of candidate

Josh Deaver who recently ended his candidacy. "May Dell Deaver is a wife, mother, and lawyer. A woman who juggles many different roles."

Deaver added, "And I like every role. After all, I chose every one of them. And I find them all to be very gratifying in interestingly diverse ways."

"Are you unhappy that you weren't up there in the debate with the other women, since your husband dropped out of the race?"

"I'm unhappy that people didn't recognize my husband for the person he is and for the qualities he could have brought to the leadership of this country. Getting his message out was a definite problem and..."

Chester interrupted the interview, with another special news bulletin. "This just in," he said sternly. "The price of gooseberry jam stock has just taken a tumble on Wall Street. Let's go to our reporter Hank Midland, who is with Milton Pippin, the leader of the national gooseberry boycott."

Hank was rather direct with his question. "Well, Mr. Pippin, are you happy now?"

Pippin shrugged. "There's still a long way to go from a few lousy points on the Stock Market to a real pattern of worker equity. Isn't it true that the UGH Network conducted a hostile take-over of the multimedia corporation that seized the newspaper chain that bought the paper mill that purchased the toothpick company that swallowed the olive import business that holds a majority of the stock in a major gooseberry producer?"

"Hey, wait a minute, I get to ask the questions here," proclaimed an indignant Hank. "Do you have a fetish for hurting an industry that produces something as delicious as gooseberry jam?"

Pippin popped, "Do you have a fetish for asking poor questions?"

COMMERCIAL BREAK: A grocer dusted around some jars of jam. He then looked up, uttering, "Pintyler's Gooseberry Jam is delicious. The jam is made from the finest berries and the finest geese, and only the finest." Suddenly, the checkers, stockers, and carry-outs burst into a song and dance routine. The melody of the song was catchy and simple. The words were predictable. "Gooseberry jam. Gooseberry jam. Pintyler's Gooseberry Jam is, oh! so damn good." Then the individual store workers each sang a verse:

"Spread it on bread."
"Spread it on meats."
"Spread it on crackers."
"Spread it on treats."
"Spread it while you're walkin'."
"Spread it while you're skippin'."
"Spread it while you're sittin'."
"Even spread it on Milton Pippin."

Then the store workers joined with voices in joyful song for a dynamic finale while romping down the store aisles. "But spread it around. Spread it around. Pintyler's Gooseberry Jam is just like a rumor. So, spread it around."

CHAPTER 13
Votes Are the Frosting on the Cake

Pollster I.M. Wigglewaggle looked as confused as the polling results he was trying to explain to anchorman

Chester Mega. He turned the sheet of paper upside down to see if that would help, but it didn't.

"Explain the findings again, would you please. For the viewers who may have been in the kitchen getting a sandwich out of the refrigerator, like I should have been," Chester requested. "In our random survey of 500 delegates, the latest UGH News and Cyberspace Diapers poll shows Andrew Chalk with 35 percent of the support, Ross Nebulan with 15 percent, and Joyce Hyphen Martindale with 10 percent," Wigglewaggle explained.

Chester, being a journalist, guessed at the mathematical total. "Well, that equals...55 percent of the support."

"Actually, 60 percent," corrected Wigglewaggle.

"Then what about the other 45 percent?"

"You mean, the other 40 percent," said Wigglewaggle, scratching his chin. "The rest of the support is going to 'None of the Above' because we only questioned delegates about the three main declared candidates."

"So, you're saying that there may be a dark horse out there somewhere?" Chester speculated.

"I don't know much about animals," Wigglewaggle replied. "But apparently a large number of delegates in our exit poll are going to vote for someone else."

"For one person? Many people? Or wigglewaggle?" Chester asked, adding that the "wigglewaggle" reference to Pollster Wigglewaggle was meant as a little election humor. "I've been waiting to say that."

Sober-sides Wigglewaggle didn't laugh. He was still puzzled about the polling outcome.

Chester continued, "And where were the delegates exiting when this exit poll was conducted?"

"They were exiting from the bar and lounge located off the convention hall lobby."

"Hmmmmm," Chester declared. "Maybe they had a bit too much to drink. Maybe they were downright smashed. Could that cause the uncommitted total to be inflated?"

Wigglewaggle's face reflected doubt. "Actually, if they were drinking, I think the total amounts for the three declared candidates are inflated."

"Makes sense," Chester commented. "What else did the poll find?"

Wigglewaggle looked at the sheet of paper. "To the question concerning what they think a dog dreams about, 85 percent answered 'food,' 10 percent answered 'sex,' and 5 percent answered 'postal carriers'."

Chester nodded.

Wigglewaggle continued, "We asked them, when they go into a convenience store for a soda that they fill up themselves, do they put the ice in their cup first or the pop first and then the ice?"

"And the results?" Chester asked curiously.

"We found that 70 percent put the ice in first, 15 percent put the pop in first and then the ice, 10 percent answered 'sex,' and five percent said they buy coffee."

"Anything more?"

Wigglewaggle eagerly answered, "Lastly, we asked the delegates, with all the news dedicated to polls, had any of them ever been included in any previous poll? A huge majority, 89 percent, said they'd never been surveyed, didn't even know anyone who had been surveyed and yet still believed most polls. Ten percent answered 'sex,' and only one percent said they'd ever been polled before." The professional pollster added, "Our poll has a margin of error of less than five percent and not more than three survey questioners padding the answers."

"Thank you, Mr. Wigglewaggle, for that insightful look

at convention delegates and their weird opinions. Now, the time has arrived for the roll call of the states and delegate vote count for the party hopefuls. Let's go down to the speaker's podium where Ameriminds Party Secretary Lana Shoemaker will call for the vote."

Secretary Shoemaker was waving to the spirited convention crowd, which cheered enthusiastically and danced and lifted signs. The convention hall was packed; there were more people gathered together than during the previous convention days. This was the day of decision. This was the day that the delegates would choose their Party's representative for president.

Secretary Shoemaker pounded the lectern with a gavel to quiet the crowd. Her voice shook nervously, as she called out, "Alabama, 55 votes."

Down in the Alabama section, a Southern belle in a gown fit for a southern cotillion answered at a microphone, "Madam Chairwoman, the great state of Alabama, first in the roll call and first to make a political statement about the future of our great and new and totally disorganized party, gives 40 votes to Andrew Chalk, 10 votes to Ross Nebulan, and 5 votes to Tom the homeless man."

Following every specific vote announcement, the delegates of that particular state would cheer.

As Shoemaker repeated the vote, Chester commented from the anchor booth, "That's a surprise. Looks like the powerful speech that was delivered by Tom the homeless man captured some attention."

Shoemaker: "Alaska, 9 votes."

A man submerged inside a parka: "Madam Chairwoman, Alaska, the largest state and most scenic, and a state which will support the gooseberry boycott, casts its 7 votes for

Tom the homeless man and 2 votes for Andrew Chalk."

After recording the vote, Shoemaker: "Arizona, 20 votes."

A senior citizen wearing typical cowboy dude garb and a bolo tie: "Arizona, where the roadrunners beep-beep and the snowbirds sleep-sleep, gives all 20 votes to Ross Nebulan, our next president."

Shoemaker: "Arkansas, 30 votes."

A farmer wearing a fake razorback hog nose: "Arkansas casts 20 votes for Andrew Chalk, 5 votes for Ross Nebulan, 3 votes for Tom the homeless man, and 2 votes for Joyce Hyphen Martindale."

Shoemaker: "California, 200 votes."

Confusion reigned in the California delegation section. In the California crowd was the original, mysterious young man in the raincoat who signed a few, quick autographs before he bolted away. Security officer Harry Hooper was not far behind. Hooper stopped in the California section to ask if anyone would like to have his autograph. When no one responded affirmatively, he got so angry that he took one delegate's head in an arm lock and forcibly signed his autograph on the back of the delegate's shirt.

Shoemaker: "California, we're waiting."

A Hollywood actor in sunglasses: "California passes."

Chester added some details from the anchor booth. "That was stage and screen actor Darren Monarch. Mr. Monarch has been in many movies. He's been nominated six times for an Oscar, has won three Oscars, and has refused two of them. His latest movie is titled 'Sex, Lies and Revolutionary War' and isn't about the Revolutionary War at all. In fact, and I am reading the synopsis, the movie is about a drifter who drifts to Chicago and falls in love with a playboy's beautiful wife. The playboy owns a large hotel, where the drifter has gotten a job as an elevator operator. And every night at 9 o'clock, the playboy's wife meets the drifter in his elevator and they have a wild, passionate encounter. And they travel up and down, from the basement to the 56th floor, with boiling passion and frequent nosebleeds. But during their affair, the woman tells the drifter that her husband won't grant her a divorce. And we have a clip from the movie at that point. Let's run the clip."

The movie segment showed two lovers embracing inside an elevator. The actress recited her lines, "So, Gustav, you must forget me and drift away, like drift wood down a glistening river of love. Just drift and drift and drift. And my heart will be there with you, like a barnacle on the side of a luxury liner." Darren Monarch, in his portrayal of the drifter, replied, "But I need this job and they wouldn't know where to send my W2 form. I can't live without you, Olive. This elevator was made for the two of us." The actress declared, "You must live without me. Because it was never meant to be for us. This elevator was never meant for me. My life is with Roger and the stairs." The actor asked, "All 48 flights of stairs?" The actress nodded and melodramatically answered, "All 48 flights."

Chester cleared his throat. "That movie sounds like a real tear-jerker. Let's go back to party secretary Lana Shoemaker and the roll call of the states."
Shoemaker: "Caucasia, 7 votes."
A white man with a middle-age spread: "Caucasia, the state of mind where group exclusion maintains the comfortable status quo, gives all its white votes to Ross Nebulan, a white man of great backward thinking."

Jeers broke out on the convention floor.

Shoemaker: "Colorado, 20 votes."

A sun-burnt ski bum in a ski outfit: "Colorado, the Rocky Mountain state, casts 10 votes for Chalk and 10 votes for Tom the homeless man.

Shoemaker: "Connecticut, 14 votes."

Boyd Larkspur, in a western-styled tuxedo, and Rosie McCoy, in a flowing white wedding gown, took turns at the microphone proudly saying, "I do" to the marriage questions of a minister. The convention crowd went wild with applause and the band played the traditional wedding song. Shoemaker smiled happily.

Chester's voice had a pleased, fatherly sound to it and, as the camera continued to show the couple in a long, romantic kiss, Chester explained, "The newlyweds will honeymoon in Cleveland, Ohio, before returning to the groom's family ranch in Montana. This was a love story that I doubt the Democratic or Republican conventions will ever match. Truly a marriage made in politics, and that sure isn't heaven, you know."

Shoemaker laughed and spoke in a motherly tone to the convention crowd, "Wouldn't it be great if that young couple came back here in four years and had a baby delivered right there on the convention floor?!"

The crowd roared its support for the idea.

Shoemaker: "Well, congratulations, Connecticut. And how about those 14 votes?"

Rosie McCoy, beaming as a happy bride, got to make the announcement: "Connecticut proudly gives all 14 votes to Tom the homeless man."

Shoemaker: "Delaware, 21 votes."

A Delaware delegate wearing a brand new jersey: "Nine votes for Andrew Chalk, 7 votes for Tom the homeless man, and 5 votes for Joyce Hyphen Martindale."

Shoemaker: "District of Columbia, 9 votes."

A delegate with a small White House replica on the top of a baseball cap: "The District of Columbia, the 51st state, and home to most presidents, wants to see Tom the homeless man get a new home. He gets all our 9 votes."

Chester commented, "There seems to be an unexpected ground-swell of support for Tom the homeless man. Who would have ever thought it! An Ameriminds candidate needs only a majority of the votes to secure the nomination."

Shoemaker: "Florida, 22 votes."

A senior citizen dressed as a beachcomber: "The great state of Florida, the state of the sweetest sunshine, the sweetest orange juice, and the meanest gators. The state that places prison executions right up there with sun-tans and other recreation casts 12 votes for Rev. Dirge and his Roaring Lions, 7 votes for Nebulan, and 3 votes for Chalk."

Shoemaker: "Georgia, 16 votes."

A cable TV executive with a southern drawl: "Georgia, with the Cherokee rose as its state flower and the brown thrasher as its state bird, casts 8 votes for Chalk and 8 votes for Nebulan."

Chester snickered, "I thought the Georgia state bird was the gnat."

Shoemaker: "Georgia, I just love Cherokee roses. They go so well with my hair. I remember when I was a little girl..."

Sydney Paine, the party chairman, gently tapped her on the shoulder, and his expression implied that she should return to the business at hand.

Shoemaker: "Guam, 2 votes."

A delegate in a sarong: "Guam, the 51st state, casts 2 votes for Andrew Chalk."

Shoemaker: "Hawaii, 7 votes."

A delegate with a lei around her neck and wearing a grass skirt: "Hawaii, the Aloha state, in the blue Pacific, passes."

Shoemaker: "Idaho, 37 votes."

A delegate in a fat potato costume: "Idaho, the spud state, which would never boycott potatoes, but will boycott gooseberries, casts its votes this way. Tom the homeless man, 30 votes; Chalk, 5 votes; and newsman Chester Mega, 2 votes."

Chester laughed, saying, "Thanks, Idaho. I like baked potatoes in their jackets."

Shoemaker: "Illinois, 80 votes."

A delegate resembling Abraham Lincoln: "Illinois, Madam Chairwoman, gives all 80 votes to its favorite son, Ross Nebulan, the next president of the United States."

Chester's voice can be heard. "Wow, that's a big boost, but expected, for Nebulan. The vote tally stands at Nebulan, 137; Chalk, 99; Tom the homeless man, 85; Dirge, 12; Hyphen Martindale, 7; and me, 2 great Idaho votes."

Shoemaker: "Indiana, 15 votes."

A tall delegate in a basketball uniform: "Ten votes for Chalk and 5 votes for Tom the homeless man."

Shoemaker: "Iowa, 10 votes."

A farmer in bib overalls: "Iowa, total area 56,032 square miles, the 25th largest state, which entered the Union on December 28, 1846, casts 9 votes for Tom the homeless man and 1 vote for Andrew Chalk."

Shoemaker: "That was very educational, Iowa. Kansas, 30 votes."

A delegate dressed as a scarecrow: "Kansas passes."

Shoemaker: "Kentucky, 31 votes."

A delegate in a chicken suit: "Thirteen votes for Tom the homeless man, 10 votes for Chalk, 5 votes for Nebulan, and 4 votes for Hyphen Martindale."

Shoemaker: "Ah, Kentucky, that amounts to 32 votes."

The delegate in the chicken suit quickly huddled with the other delegates.

Chester broke in. "Let's quickly go down to the convention floor with Saphira Pitchfork, who has a special guest. Saphira, who have you got there?"

Saphira was all smiles. "Chester, with me is Tessie Schafer, a delegate from Illinois. And she was Ross Nebulan's first grade teacher at the Sunny-Playtime School for the Rich and Arrogant in his suburban hometown in Illinois."

"Yes," the elderly woman said in a high and squeaky voice. "That's correct. His very first teacher. And I knew he would be great someday. He made the best N's. They were so straight and neat. I would think that it was from his practice of printing the name Nebulan. There are two N's, you know, in that name. His L's were also very good. And he printed numbers excellently. I don't think I ever saw a time when he let his 6's swim. Always nice, neat curves, properly on the line."

"Did you have any disciplinary problems with little Ross?" asked Saphira, wanting to get to the juicy stuff.

"Well, he was a very good boy. Let's see, only once did I scold him. It was...yes...it was during the milk break with Peter Dobie, the little boy with the pet grasshopper. Yes, I caught little Ross sticking a piece of chalk up Peter's nose. But it was all right. Little Ross didn't even break the chalk."

Saphira summed it up, "How ironic that he is in a race

with Chalk right this minute."

The Kentucky delegate was finally ready to correct his earlier announcement. "That should be only 3 votes for Ms. Hyphen Martindale."

Shoemaker: "Louisiana, 14 votes."

A delegate in a wild Mardi Gras outfit: "Louisiana, where the Mardi Gras draws millions of people each year. Round tickets to New Orleans are on sale right now. We cast 6 votes for Chalk, 4 votes for Nebulan, and 4 votes for Rev. Dirge."

Shoemaker: "Maine, 9 votes."

A delegate dressed as a lobster fisherman: "Maine wants some of those Mardi Gras airplane tickets. Maine casts 6 votes for Tom the homeless man, 2 votes for Chalk, and 1 vote for the young man in the raincoat."

Shoemaker: "Ameriminds Abroad, 16 votes."

A short, green delegate with antennae and dressed in a three-piece suit: "From places where gooseberries are free to live their lives without fear of harvest, we Ameriminds abroad cast 8 votes for Tom the homeless man, 4 votes for Milton Pippin the great gooseberry boycott leader, and 4 votes for Fixip2 5#bwops87."

Shoemaker: "Maryland, 25 votes."

A delegate in a Chesapeake Bay blue crab costume: "Maryland, proudly named for a woman, gives 20 votes to Joyce Hyphen Martindale and 5 votes to Tom the homeless man."

Shoemaker: "Massachusetts, 30 votes."

A delegate resembling President Kennedy with a similar Bostonian accent: "Massachusetts proudly gives 25 votes to Tom the homeless man and 5 votes to Andrew Chalk."

Shoemaker: "Michigan, 85 votes."

An auto worker delegate: "Michigan passes."

Shoemaker: "Minnesota, 22 votes."

A delegate dressed as a fisherman with a mosquito net protecting his face: "Minnesota gives 12 votes to Tom the homeless man and 10 votes to Andrew Chalk."

Shoemaker: "Mississippi, 20 votes."

A beauty pageant contestant: "Mississippi votes 'nay'."

Shoemaker flinched. "Mississippi, we are voting for candidates for the party's presidential nomination. Please count up your votes."

Chester Mega broke in. "UGH News has just learned that candidate Andrew Chalk's cousin's godmother has died of shopping mall exhaustion. Let's go quickly down to reporter Hank Midland who is with Mr. Chalk's campaign manager, Barney Baylor."

Baylor read a short statement that was approved by candidate Chalk. "The Chalk campaign is greatly shocked and saddened. Shopping mall exhaustion is a health problem that is sweeping this nation in alarming proportions. Shopping mall exhaustion now ranks as the third leading cause of death for people with incomes above $500,000. Candidate Chalk pledges his utmost to do something about it, so a tragedy of this nature will never happen again. Delegates who believe that a shopping mall experience should be a happy experience, should vote for Andrew Chalk."

Reporter Hank Midland quickly concluded, "The shopping mall contingent, which has been consistently supportive of Ross Nebulan, could respond sympathetically to the Chalk campaign.
We'll have to wait and see. Back to the roll call vote."

The Mississippi beauty pageant contestant: "We're split. Ten votes for the wonderful and sexy Andrew Chalk, and the men are acting like jerks and want to give their 10 votes to Ross Nebulan."

Shoemaker: "Missouri, 10 votes."

Former candidate Josh Deaver of Missouri: "The delegates here are the greatest people in the world. They say they still want to vote for me. So, that's 9 votes for Deaver and I give my one vote to Tom the homeless man."

Shoemaker: "Montana, 25 votes."

A cowgirl delegate: "Montana, Big Sky country, congratulates our favorite son, Boyd Larkspur and his beautiful wife Rosie McCoy on their knot-tying, and we give 14 votes to Tom the homeless man and 11 votes to Andrew Chalk."

Shoemaker: "Nebraska, 40 votes."

A delegate in an ear-of-corn costume: "Nebraska, with the world's greatest football team, casts 26 votes for Tom the homeless man, 10 votes for Andrew Chalk, and 4 votes for the Orange Bowl."

Shoemaker: "Go, Big Red. Okay...Nevada, 10 votes."

A delegate in a glittering chorus line costume with a feather boa: "The sparkling state of Nevada would like to bet...I mean, casts its 10 votes for Andrew Chalk, who's welcome to visit us any time."

Shoemaker: "New Hampshire, 36 votes."

A delegate in a heavy coat and ear muffs, with a tin of maple syrup: "New Hampshire, Madam Chairwoman, passes."

Shoemaker: "New Jersey, 30 votes."

A delegate in a chemical laboratory apron and protective eye-goggles: "New Jersey gives 20 votes to Andrew Chalk and 10 votes to Tom the homeless man."

Shoemaker: "New Mexico, 20 votes."

A delegate with a strand of jalapeno peppers around her

neck: "New Mexico gives 10 votes to Chalk and 10 votes to Tom the homeless man."

Shoemaker: "New York, 170 votes."

A rude delegate: "Get out of the way because we're passing."

After a frown for New York, Shoemaker continued: "North Carolina, 10 votes."

A delegate dressed as a long cigarette: "North Carolina...(the delegates cough)...gives Nebulan 5 votes and Chalk 5 votes."

Shoemaker: "North Dakota, 9 votes."

A delegate with an accordion: "Six votes to Tom the homeless man and 3 votes to Andrew Chalk."

Shoemaker: "Ohio, 20 votes."

A factory worker with a dollar bill taped over one eye, to signify a "buck eye": "Ohio casts 10 votes for Chalk and 10 votes for Nebulan. And we support the gooseberry boycott."

Shoemaker: "Oklahoma, 11 votes."

A wealthy oil executive: "Oklahoma, where the oil and tornadoes run wild, gives 6 votes to Chalk and 5 votes for Nebulan."

Chester interrupted to report the vote count. "Chalk now leads with 238; Tom the homeless man, 235; Nebulan, 176; Hyphen Martindale, 30; Dirge, 16; Deaver, 9; Pippin, 4; Fixip2 5#bwops87, 4; Orange Bowl, 4; two great Idaho votes for me; and one vote for the young man in the raincoat.

Shoemaker: "Oregon, 18 votes."

A young woman in a raincoat: "Oregon gives all 18 votes to the young man in the raincoat. Raincoats are our life."

Shoemaker: "Pennsylvania, 80 votes."

A factory worker with a pink slip: "Pennsylvania gives all

80 votes to its favorite son, Andrew Chalk."

Shoemaker: "Puerto Rico, 7 votes."

A delegate in a tank top and shorts: "Puerto Rico, the 51st state, gives 5 votes for Nebulan and 2 votes for Chalk."

Shoemaker: "Rhode Island, 8 votes."

A short delegate carrying a large magnifying glass: "We're small but we're rich. All 8 votes to rich Ross Nebulan."

Shoemaker: "South Carolina, 17 votes."

A delegate dressed as a Confederate soldier: "South Carolina would like to give all its 17 votes to Jefferson Davis, but he's dead. So, we give them to Rev. Dirge."

Shoemaker: "South Dakota, 10 votes."

A delegate in bib overalls: "South Dakota, the great state of Mount Rushmore, gives all 10 votes to Tom the homeless man."

Chester interrupted briefly. "I read in one of those tabloid magazines that if you go to the back side of Mount Rushmore, you can see the backs of the presidents' heads."

Shoemaker: "Television, 50 votes."

Chester interrupted again. "This is an interesting delegate group that consists of people watching the convention by TV. It's similar to the 'distance learning' concept, only it is a lot of 'distance' and very little 'learning.' The Republican convention also wants to utilize the concept."

A "talking head" on a TV screen: "Television, the 51st state, proudly casts 20 votes for Tom the homeless man, 20 votes for the Make-Me-Happy Deodorant Roll-0n Woman, 5 votes for the heroic young man in the raincoat, and 5 votes for the reruns of the James Cash Cathcart public execution."

Shoemaker: "Tennessee, 27 votes."

An Elvis impersonator: "Tennessee, Madam

Chairwoman, gives 11 votes to Tom the homeless man, 10 votes to Andrew Chalk, 4 votes to Ross Nebulan, and 2 votes to Rev. Dirge."

Shoemaker: "Texas, 92 votes."

A Texas cowboy: "The proud state of Texas, the biggest state in the Union despite what Alaska thinks, proudly passes."

Shoemaker: "Utah, 23 votes."

A student Mormon missionary sitting on a bicycle: "Utah casts 12 votes for Nebulan, 9 votes for Chalk, and 2 votes for Ross Nebulan's first grade teacher, Mrs. Schafer."

Shoemaker: "Vermont, 8 votes."

A delegate dressed as a moose: "Six votes to Tom the homeless man and 2 votes to Andrew Chalk."

Shoemaker: "Virginia, 16 votes."

A delegate in a colonial costume: "The Rev. Dirge, 8 votes; Chalk, 6 votes; and Tom the homeless man, 2 votes."

Shoemaker: "Virgin Islands, 3 votes."

A delegate in a flowered tourist shirt and swimming trunks: "The Virgin Islands, the 51st state, happily gives its 3 votes to the man who knows what's great about the Virgin Islands, Andrew Chalk."

Shoemaker: "Washington, 11 votes."

A delegate carrying a large, inflated, toy salmon: "Washington supports the gooseberry boycott. And we cast 6 votes for Tom the homeless man, 4 votes for Andrew Chalk, and one vote for the young man in the raincoat."

Shoemaker: "West Virginia, 8 votes."

A coal miner: "West Virginia gives all its 8 votes to the great Tom the homeless man."

Shoemaker: "Wisconsin, 50 votes."

A delegate dressed in a big cheese costume: "Wisconsin, where dairy cows also vote, casts 30 votes for Tom the homeless man, 15 votes for Andrew Chalk, and 5 votes for Joyce Hyphen Martindale."

Shoemaker: "Wyoming, 70 votes."

A cowgirl wearing typical western clothes, including batwing chaps, and with a branch of tumbleweed stuck in her hair: "The great state of Wyoming, always last in the roll call, but first in the minds of people who know that the best is saved for last; the state of fresh air, fresh water, and fresh cowboys; the state where the buffalo roam and the deer and the antelope play poker; the state that was first in the nation and world to give women the right to vote and to hold public office and has some soreheads who are still upset about it; and the state that's practically empty because most of its residents are here as delegates, casts 50 votes for Tom the homeless man, 10 votes for Andrew Chalk, 9 votes for Ross Nebulan, and 1 vote for Joyce Hyphen Martindale."

Chester quickly reviewed the vote count. "And here's the tally, up to now, with states that previously passed to be called upon next. Remember that the Ameriminds Party's nominee needs only a majority of the 1,665 votes. And there are some surprising results, as Tom the homeless man, I'm sure surprised himself, has come on strong in delegate support. It is a race between him and Andrew Chalk. But there are still some big vote amounts yet to come. Here's how it stands now: Chalk, 379; Tom the homeless man, 378; Nebulan, 214; Dirge, 43; Hyphen Martindale, 36; the young man in the raincoat, 25; the Make-Me-Happy Deodorant Roll-On Woman, 20; Deaver, 9; execution reruns, 5; Pippin, 4; Fixip2 5#bwops87, 4; Orange Bowl, 4; first-grade teacher Schafer, 2; and me, 2 great Idaho votes. California, which is next, may be the one that gives the nominee a whopping lead and thus determines the outcome."

Shoemaker: "California, 120 votes."
Darren Monarch, the handsome Hollywood actor in
sunglasses: "California, where anything can happen and
usually does; where silly, short-term fads start and then
sweep across the nation, taking about 10 years before they
become popular elsewhere; where acting and politics go
hand-in-hand and sometimes foot-in-mouth; and the state
that will boycott not only gooseberries, but also potato
chips, fur coats, turtle soup, and dalmatian colorization,
casts 38 votes for Tom the homeless man; 27 votes for
Andrew Chalk, 10 votes for Fixip2 5#bwops87--whoever
or whatever that is--,10 votes for Joyce Hyphen Martindale,
10 votes for Ross Nebulan, 10 votes for the young man in
the raincoat, 8 votes for Mandy of Generation X-Crement,
3 votes for superstar Charla Willow, 2 votes for the Make-
Me-Happy Deodorant Roll-On Woman, 1 vote for body-
piercing, and I vote for myself, of course, so that's 1 vote
for Darren Monarch."
Chester explained, "California split its vote so much that
it will take some other state to give a nominee a victorious
outcome."
Shoemaker: "Hawaii, 7 votes."
The spokeswoman from Hawaii: "Hawaii passes."
Shoemaker: "Kansas, 30 votes."
The scarecrow: "Twenty votes for Chalk and 10 votes for
Rev. Dirge."
Shoemaker: "Michigan, 85 votes."
A Michigan delegate: "Sorry Madam Chairwoman, but
Michigan passes again."
Shoemaker: "New Hampshire, 36 votes."
A New Hampshire delegate: "New Hampshire passes."

Shoemaker wiped her perspiring face with a hankie. The tension in the convention mounted.

Shoemaker: "New York, 170 votes."

A rude New York delegate: "About time. The great state of New York, the state of greatness, the state of people, the state of power, the state of confusion--a little humor there, get it. Well, if California is going to boycott gooseberries, we will boycott gooseberries and California. Beat that! New York casts 80 votes for Tom the homeless man though he dresses like trash; 70 votes for Andrew Chalk though he wasn't gentlemanly enough to meet with all our women delegates; 10 votes for Joyce Hyphen Martindale who's got a big mouth; and 10 votes for that nauseating Mandy."

Shoemaker: "Texas, 92 votes."

A Texas delegate: "Texas, Madam Chairman, the biggest state in the Union despite what Alaska thinks, the state where our outhouses are bigger than the capitol buildings in other states..."

Shoemaker interrupted. "I've been to Texas and you need outhouses that big." Laughter erupted throughout the convention.

The Texas delegate continued with a surly tone: "Fifty votes for James Cash Cathcart's prison warden, 20 votes for Andrew Chalk, 13 votes for hometown gal Joyce Hyphen Martindale, and 9 votes for the Rev. Dirge. We refuse to boycott gooseberries. And we have prisons that would give Tom the homeless man a home."

Hisses and boos were uttered by other convention delegates.

Shoemaker hammered the gavel on the top of the lectern to regain order. "Please," requested Shoemaker, "Can we get along here?"

As the camera remained fixed upon Shoemaker, Chester's

voice could be heard, "It takes a lot of patience during one of these conventions. Just rounding up the delegates for the vote count can be a big chore, especially for the bigger delegations. I can remember times at other conventions when delegates would say they were going to get a drink of water and then reappear several days later with a major hangover. They apparently voted for beer."

Some of the women delegates screamed with joy at the appearance of candidate Andrew Chalk in the wings of the speaker's platform. Chester noted the arrival, "Andrew Chalk is making his first appearance here at the convention and it is causing quite a stir. I don't see his wife, Cassie, with him."

Chalk smiled and waved as Shoemaker pounded the gavel again.

Shoemaker: "Michigan, 85 votes."

A Michigan delegate: "Fifty votes to Tom the homeless man, 30 votes for Chalk, 4 votes for Hyphen Martindale, and 1 vote for Mandy."

Delegates were cheering with more enthusiasm as the vote counts neared a dramatic finale. Andrew Chalk and Tom the homeless man were now even in the tabulation. Each had 546 votes.

Shoemaker: "New Hampshire, 36 votes."

A New Hampshire delegate: "Eighteen votes for Andrew Chalk and 18 votes for Tom the homeless man."

The convention crowd gave a large gasp of excitement. The vote was still split and it would take Hawaii, with its odd-number of votes, to make the final decision. The drummer in the convention band provided a quick drum roll. Candidate Andrew Chalk waved to the crowd from the back of the speaker's platform. He was confident, as he remembered sleeping with at least one woman from

Hawaii. He tried to spot his wife, so he could have her stand, smiling, at his side, but he couldn't see her. Chalk's campaign manager Barney Baylor, who had studied the voter information tabulated earlier, was smiling. Baylor showed Chalk a clipboard with the tallied figures. Hawaii had two women delegates and five men delegates. Chalk had won over the women's votes and had the pledges of two of the men delegates. That would make him the winner by one vote.

Shoemaker's voice quivered. "Hawaii, 7 votes."

Chester broke in. "Let's go down to reporter Trixie Spaniel for a giant news scoop."

Trixie Spaniel was standing in front of harried Hawaiian delegates who were chattering and shrugging and looking incredibly confused. "Chester," Trixie began, "You aren't going to believe this. Apparently, two of the male Hawaiian delegates pledged to voting for Chalk are now unaccounted for. One of the female members of the delegation last saw them at the Chalk hotel. And they aren't sure if they've returned to the convention complex."

The report was true. Back at the hotel suite, Cassie Chalk was making use of the accommodations, now that her husband, the candidate, was at the convention. Flowered Hawaiian shirts, swimming trunks and other clothing, strewn across the bedroom carpet, created a path to the bed. Mrs. Chalk knew the mystery of the missing Hawaiian delegates. The two virile men were right there with her in the large, soft bed.

Secretary Shoemaker couldn't give the Hawaii delegation any more time. "Hawaii, I'm sorry, but we need your votes."

The Hawaii chairwoman, with tears in her eyes, reported, "Two of us vote for that wonderful gentleman Andrew Chalk and three of the delegates vote for Tom the homeless man and..." The woman stopped, as the convention crowd seemed to hold its breath and a complete silence settled across the vast sea of anxious convention participants.

Shoemaker questioned: "And the other two votes?"

The Hawaii chairwoman shrugged.

Shoemaker rendered the final verdict: "And two abstentions. Tom the homeless man wins the nomination."

Pandemonium swept the convention hall. The crowd cheered wildly. Millions of colorful balloons fell from the rafters of the hall. The band loudly played the "Stars and Stripes Forever."

Delegates danced and shouted and made goofy faces at the TV cameras.

History had been made. Their new nominee, the first presidential nominee of the new Ameriminds Party, had been chosen for all of the world to see and it was Tom the homeless man.

Up in the UGH News anchor booth, only Chester Mega's head could be seen, as the rest of him and his news desk were buried in balloons. "There you have it. Tomorrow's front-page headlines. Tom the homeless man to lead the Ameriminds Party. What a political season! What a political feat! A man without any campaign funding, no campaign committee, no negative ads, and no sharp disposable razor rises to the top. Oh, what a story! Only in America, folks. Only in America."

Reporter Hank Midland was with candidate Andrew Chalk. "Mr. Chalk, it was a close race, but no cigar. What happened? How'd a novice like Tom the homeless man pick up such steam?"

Chalk didn't answer. His expression translated into shock and disbelief.

The convention crowd started to chant for "Tom" over and over. "We want Tom, we want Tom, we want Tom..."

Reporter Trixie Spaniel stood on the speaker's platform, and the TV camera pointed toward former candidate Josh Deaver who was talking with Montana cowboy Boyd Larkspur, still in his western-styled tuxedo; Boyd's new wife Rosie McCoy, wearing her flowing white wedding gown; Party Chairman Sydney Paine; and Party Secretary Lana Shoemaker.

"There seems to be a problem here," Trixie explained. "No one knows where Tom the homeless man has gone. I guess we could say that Tom the homeless man is a political prodigy of former candidate Deaver. After all, Deaver had allowed him time to speak to the convention and that event has been heralded by spin doctors and witch doctors alike as a turning point for delegates. From what I can hear, Deaver thinks he knows where Tom the homeless man is, but he needs someone to keep the convention crowd occupied. Apparently, the convention newlyweds, Boyd and Rosie, have agreed to take on that duty."

Deaver hurriedly left the platform, as Boyd and Rosie approached the microphone at the lectern. The convention crowd continued to chant for Tom, but Boyd and Rosie raised their arms and motioned for silence. Eventually, the cheering decreased, and Boyd told the crowd, "Tom the homeless man will be here in a minute or so. In the meantime, Rosie and I would like lead all of you in a rendition of...of...that old gospel song, 'We Shall Gather At the River.' How about it?"

However, Rosie leaned against Boyd, whispering in his ear, "We need more time than that. We need something longer, so Josh can find Tom the homeless man."

Boyd nodded in agreement, glad that his new bride was so smart. He cleared his throat. "Better yet, here's an old gospel tune that I bet you all know and love. Let's join in and make this convention the most musically festive in history."

The delegates cheered, and the convention band waited for Boyd's cue. Boyd started the song, "Ninety-nine bottles of beer on the wall, 99 bottles of beer. Take one down and pass it around. Ninety-eight bottles of beer on the wall."

Rosie took the next verse and eagerly motioned to the crowd to join her, which happened with enthusiastically. "Ninety-eight bottles of beer on the wall, 98 bottles of beer. Take one down and pass it around. Ninety-seven bottles of beer on the wall..."

CHAPTER 14
From Dumpster to Campaign Trail

Josh Deaver's suspicions of the whereabouts of Tom the homeless man proved to be correct. Deaver found Tom outside the back of the convention building, in the dark alley, shifting through items in a dumpster.

Tom's head was practically inside the dumpster as he used a stick from a broken tree branch to poke through the garbage bags.

"Finding anything?" Josh asked to get Tom's attention.

Tom pulled back from the dumpster and nodded to his

friend. "It's amazing how much unconscious compassion there can be in a dumpster," Tom replied. "The wasted food could feed a lot of people in need."

"You know that the convention kitchen and banquet table is open to you, as a guest and convention speaker," Josh said, as a way of making certain Tom knew he was welcome there.

Tom nodded. "I know that. I've never eaten so well in recent times. But it didn't feel right, either. I kept thinking about all of the people out on the streets. And I got worried that, because I had a good meal, I would forget about the others, just as lots of comfortable, fortunate people do now." Tom asked, "Do you think I'll ever become like that? I mean, I don't want to be forgetful."

Josh smiled, but his eyes were sad. "I don't think you'll ever forget. I think you'll remember, I think you'll always want to help others, and I think you'll also be thankful for what you have. Those feelings go together for the better people in this world. And I think you're one of those people."

Tom bowed his head, embarrassed by the compliments, humbled by the confidence.

Josh continued, "And there are lots of people in that big convention hall tonight who agree with me."

Tom looked up with curious surprise at Josh.

"Yes," Josh answered to Tom's expression, "The majority of the delegates have decided. They want you to be their candidate. They want you to take your ideas to the Washington and the White House."

"Huh?!" Tom speechlessly uttered.

"The nomination. The presidential nomination is yours if you want it," Josh explained.

Tom turned away, confused and frightened. "I...I...I can't

do that. I don't know a thing about politics. I don't know a thing about campaigning. I don't even have a tie. You deserve to be the nominee. You are a good man, Josh Deaver, and you are best for the country."

Josh smiled and replied, "It's not my time, Tom. It's your time. This moment in history is yours. And, heck, I have plenty of ties. You can borrow them." Then Josh added honestly, "I don't want to imply that it would be easy. It won't be easy, Tom. It will probably be the hardest thing you've ever done." Josh stopped and corrected himself, "No, I didn't mean that. Being homeless is the hardest thing a person could ever do. Running for president is a different kind of adversity."

Tom didn't know what to say.

"The Democrats have the presidency, the Republicans have the Congress, the Independents have the Texas panhandle, and the big corporations have all of them," Josh said. "But you have something they don't have, Tom. You are real and they are molded plastic. You care and they watch the polls. You know what it's like to be financially hurting and they haven't got a clue. That means something, Tom."

"It means I probably can't get elected," Tom said with a laugh.

"But it sure could be fun trying," Josh answered. "How about it?"

Tom paused for a moment and looked up at the stars in the night sky. Finally, Tom turned to Josh and said, "Well, I'll do it under one condition."

"What's that?"

"That you'd be willing to serve as my Secretary of the Interior if I win."

Josh smiled widely. "I agree."

"And my campaign consultant?"

"I'd be a campaign 'insultant' if that's what you wanted," Josh said and they both laughed. Josh threw his arm around Tom's shoulder, as they began to walk to the convention's back-door entrance.

"Would your wife be willing to serve as a proxy first lady?"

"You'd have to ask her about that," Josh stated. "I always thought she'd make a great one. And who'd be your choice as a vice presidential running mate? You know, someone who could get you some media attention."

"Well, I always thought the Make-Me-Happy Deodorant Roll-On Woman possessed great charisma..."

CHAPTER 15
Revelations of the Young Man in the Raincoat

COMMERCIAL: The camera caught the car salesman setting a bumper back into place on a car. He abruptly jumped up, saying, "A great little model, this car. See how easy it is to change bumperstickers. Brothers and sisters, at Ted's Automotive Global City, we have a sharp little model from 1975 through 1990, meaning it has a different piece for every year." He looked skyward, figuring. "That's at least sixteen pieces. And this car comes from Pasadena. Now you may think, 'Oh, that little, old lady from Pasadena routine.' No way! Our cars have stereos, not stereotypes, you know. This car did not belong to a little, old lady from Pasadena. No, it didn't. It belonged to a little, old man from Pasadena. So, come on down and take a test drive, as long as it's around the block." He slammed the car door and the impact made the bumper fall off. "And remember, this car has a 10-mile guarantee." After the salesman lifted the bumper back into its correct position, the four doors dropped to the ground and the radio antenna curled. The salesman pointed at the camera, "But for YOU, a 5-mile guarantee."

SECOND COMMERCIAL: The Make-Me-Happy Deodorant Roll-On Woman was sitting behind a desk in a room designed to resemble the Oval Office in the White House. She gingerly applied deodorant to her under-arms. "Politics as usual? Don't sweat it." She blew a kiss sensuously at the camera.

Meanwhile, back at the convention, anchorman Chester Mega was ready to greet the viewers as the background sound of singing from the convention participants could be heard. "Sixty-five bottles of beer on the wall, 65 bottles of beer. Take one down and pass it around. Sixty-four bottles of beer on the wall..."

Chester was optimistic. "Welcome back, everyone. The tension is growing and the singing is getting worse, as everyone here at the Ameriminds convention awaits hearing from its newly proclaimed leader, Tom the homeless man. Let's take a minute to hear from the people who had a lot to do with this convention, keeping it in top shape while so many others were trying to trash it. Let's go to Saphira Pitchfork."

Saphira was standing in the convention hall's main office with two convention workers. She may have chosen the assignment to get away from the singing on the convention floor.

Saphira introduced the woman first. "This is Gertrude Dryer, the official head physician for the convention. Dr.

Dryer, has your crew been busy during the last several days?"

Dr. Dryer asked for clarification. "You mean with patients?"

Saphira nodded.

Dr. Dryer flipped to a page in a notebook and pulled a pen from its tucked position above her right ear. "Well, the convention has gone very well in terms of health. We've hardly used up the stock of tongue depressors. Delegates have reported the following cases: 635 black eyes, 354 bloody noses, 200 cases of indigestion, 174 cases of insomnia, 70 panic attacks, 56 broken arms, 37 cases of fever, 20 cases of dizziness, 15 cases of exhaustion, 10 cases of beer...oh, excuse me." The physician blushed, rapidly scratching out the line with her pen. "Five cases of nausea, one toothache, 10 'reported' cases of kleptomania, 789 cases of intoxication, one case of hives because of an excessive amount of gooseberry jam, and one case of hoof-and-mouth disease."

Saphira tested some of her investigative skills. "Did any of the politicians make requests for condoms?"

Dr. Dryer was stern. "Oh, we can't release that information. You'd have to make a request about that to the CIA through the Freedom of Information Act. And the CIA is a bottomless pit of undisclosed information. Most requests never get anywhere. It's national security, you know."

Saphira turned to her other side to interview a convention maintenance man. "This is Pop Shug, who's the supervisor of clean-up for the convention. Pop, can you give us the dirt about the dirt?"

"Sure can. The damned fools! Runnin' around, chatterin' and clutterin' up the joint," complained the janitor. "My crew worked night 'n day to keep this joint from becoming a regular pigs' sty. We broke quite a few brooms over the heads of litter bugs who refused to bend over and pick up what they'd dropped. Brooms don't come cheap, you know."

"I'm curious," Saphira asked with interest. "As a convention worker, who do you support?"

"Support?" responded Pop Shug. "I support a wife and four kids." He stared at the camera. "Hi, Mother. And kids. I'll be home late again tonight." He waved.

Back at the convention hall, Boyd and Rosie were cheerfully leading the delegates through another song verse. "Forty-two bottles of beer on the wall, 42 bottles of beer. Take one down and pass it around. Forty-one bottles of beer on the wall..."

Reporter Mike Troy cornered Barney Baylor, the campaign manager of losing candidate Andrew Chalk, and it wasn't an easy task for the reporter since the huge-framed Baylor was visibly distraught and three sheets to the wind because of a near self-drowning with liquor.

Troy asked the usual bad question. "How do you feel at this moment?"

"As champagne manager, at this moment I feel tingly. All of those champagne bubbles are making my eyes water and my nose explode," Baylor explained slowly.

"That's too bad."

"Nothing of the kind. I enjoy every bubble." Baylor snorted. His pulpy hand grabbed Troy's shoulder. "Go ahead. Question me any ask...I mean, ask me any question..."

The reporter made a quick side-step as the falling body of

the drunken campaign manager toppled to the floor.

Troy sat down on the loudly snoring man's large hip. The reporter explained to the viewers, "Politics is a lot like sports. There's the ecstasy of victory and the agony of defeat.Let's go to reporter Bella Wing who's in the front lobby with convention gardener Cecil Greengrow."

Bella asked the gardener for a quick description of the beautiful landscaping throughout the convention building.

"In the lobby alone, we have evergreens, junipers and spruce. Also, zinnias, bachelor's buttons, glads, baby's breath, roses and tulips," Greengrow replied.

"It is lovely."

"We use rocks and rock gardens throughout the complex. You probably recognize the jade. Well, there's about everything else here, too. From sandstone to lava rock, from coal to quartz. Of course, the diamonds are kept in the vault. And this," the gardener pointed to a layer of rock used to trim an area of evergreens, "is gneiss."

"It sure is nice," agreed Bella.

The gardener emphasized, "And it is all sprayed with stinky fox urine to reduce the potential of theft, unwarranted rock-collecting or people tiptoeing through the tulips."

Bella turned to the camera, "Rock landscaping like this should not be taken just for granite." Bella held the microphone in front of the gardener who eagerly got to say, "Back to you, Chester."

UGH News anchorman Chester Mega had his back to the camera as he was using binoculars to peer through the anchor booth's broken window at the speaker's platform. Chester was singing with the convention crowd. "Twenty-seven bottles of beer on the wall, 27 bottles of beer. Take one down and pass it around. Twenty-six bottles of beer on the wall..."

The convention crowd began to cheer. The singing faded, replaced by loud, exuberant applause and celebration. Tom the homeless man, accompanied by Josh Deaver, had arrived at the platform.

Tom was greeted jubilantly by Boyd and Rosie, Sydney Paine, and Lana Shoemaker. Andrew Chalk, Ross Nebulan and Joyce Hyphen Martindale joined the group upon the podium, mainly to wave at TV cameras and friends.

In the excitement, only security officer Harry Hooper, in the right wing of the platform stage, noticed the young man in the raincoat suddenly bolt from the left wing of the platform toward the candidates.

Harry realized this was the moment for which the young man in the raincoat had been waiting. Just as Harry had worried. Harry also realized that he was too far away to stop the young man in the raincoat. As the security officer dashed forward, he stumbled and fell. On the carpet, he quickly brandished his revolver from the holster inside his coat. Harry yelled loud enough to cause all of the people on the speaker's platform to freeze with alarm, "Look out, he's got a gun!"

The young man in the raincoat pushed Boyd into the arms of Rosie and took center-stage near the microphone as the others on the platform drew back in terror, impeding any clear shot Harry might have had.

The convention crowd uttered a unison gasp and the TV cameras quickly moved in for a close-up of the scene.

Harry rammed his revolver back into its holster, jumped to his feet and rushed forward. He took a flying leap toward the young man in the raincoat, however, his target abruptly moved and Harry sailed over the front of the speaker's platform. Luckily, he avoided injury by accidentally landing upon several plump delegates below.

Breathing deeply with his chest visibly pulsating beneath the raincoat, the young man in the raincoat gazed skyward, enjoying his moment of self-gratifying rapture. He stood triumphantly at the center of attention before the entire convention crowd, the TV cameras, and the watching world. He turned around, seized the bottom end of his coat, and lifted it to moon the TV cameras and convention.

The convention crowd gasped again, as the young man in the raincoat remained in a mooning position.

Then, satisfied with his stunt, the young man in raincoat straightened up, turned to face the cameras and delegates, and let his coat fall from his shoulders to the floor. He stood there, completely naked, as he started to wave a hand.

The convention delegates gasped in unison again.

Delegates in the front, directly below the speaker's platform pushed the crowd back in a panic that the young man—now out of the raincoat might—might release a urine stream upon them.

One near-sighted delegate fearfully asked, "It that a gun? Does he have a gun?"

A variety of comments spilled from the lips of surprised convention participants.

Chester Mega: "Holy blue dot!"

Matilda, the president of the Young Man in the Raincoat fan club: "My hero!"

Mandy: "Tablets."

Joyce Hyphen Martindale, unimpressed: "So what?"

Harry Hooper, dazed and babbling: "The license plate. Get the license plate."

Milton Pippin: "But does he support the gooseberry boycott?"

Rev. Dirge: "It's the end of the world!"

Charla Willow, to a grinning Joey the cameraman: "No need for computer graphic enhancement there."

Realizing that the young man no longer in the raincoat wasn't carrying a gun or dangerous after all, the group on the podium then joined at the front, waving to the convention delegates and media cameras.

In a row, there were Lana Shoemaker, Sydney Paine, Josh Deaver, Tom the homeless nominee, the naked young man, Boyd and Rosie, Andrew Chalk, Ross Nebulan, and Joyce Hyphen Martindale, smiling and waving to the crowd. Of course, the media cameras for home viewers had to apply a "blue dot" over the naked man's private parts. The convention crowd cheered excitedly.

The UGH News camera returned to Chester Mega at the anchor desk. Forcing a fatherly smile, Chester said, "And folks, remember, this is just the beginning of the campaign season. And we'll be here to report it all. Have a great evening."

THE END

ABOUT THE AUTHOR...

D.L. Roberts is an author who has worked as a journalist, newspaper editor, and mass communication professor. You can write to him at bowpost@aol.com.

His novels, in paperback and e-book form, include:

Comedies—That's Funny: Three Comedies, The Monster of Tomb Lake, That's Different, Audience (Theater Seats), and The Unconventional Convention.

Humorous Short Story Collections—Sage Street and The Honor of Your Presence.

Drama—A Stranger in Town and A Portrait of Tom

Science Fiction—Secrets (A Space Adventure)

Horror—The Wolves and Short Stories

Romance Short Stories—A Man, a Woman and a Story